A SWEET VOICE

MARGO HANSEN

A SWEET VOICE

All Scripture quotations in this book are taken from the King James Version of the Bible.

This novel is a work of fiction. Names, descriptions, entities, and incidents included in the story are products of the author's imagination. Any resemblance to actual persons, events, and entities is entirely coincidental.

Published in the United States of America

1. Fiction / Action & Adventure
2. Fiction / Christian / Historical Romance

In memory of my aunt
Eldora Lunde,
who loved Ulen and
worked to preserve its history

To my Ulen relatives,
past and present

To my husband Bruce,
who fills my life with songs

Acknowledgments

I lived the first year of my life in Ulen, Minnesota, the setting for this story. It is where I was fortunate to come when my family *went home* for visits to my grandparents' farm.

To my Ulen cousins: Carol, Steve, Collene, Ann, and Alan. What great memories I have of playing with all of you! The sack swing, the playhouse, the hayloft, the music room, holiday meals, Christmas programs, Ma and Pa, the gum tree, lefse, Easter breakfast, Aunt Irene, Archie and Blanche, Uncle Ted, trips to Flom, our names in the *Ulen Union* because we had supper at your house...the years went by much too quickly. I'm so glad I got to spend some of them with you.

To my Ulen friends: Even though the setting is your town, you may not recognize it as such. The time is 1893, and I tried to stay true to what happened during that time; however, since my story is fiction, I have taken liberties. For example: there is no record that the owners of the Austinson & Asleson General Store ever left it in the hands of another family while they took a vacation, and there was no second story to the building. The City Hotel was not sold to my fictitious family, the Prescotts. I added the dress and millinery shop a little early; it didn't actually open until four years later. Other discrepancies you may find, but I hope you will overlook them and enjoy the story and remember the rich heritage given us by our ancestors.

To all my readers: Thank you for once again coming on an adventure with me. I pray that the message of Salvation given in this book will reach a lost soul and that it will be an encouragement to all of the matchless Grace of God.

Preface

By 1893, Ulen was already seven years old. The small community boasted of merchants, hardware stores, blacksmith shops, grain elevators, a hotel, the railroad, a post office, schools, churches, and a newspaper. Farmers endured despite grasshopper invasions, droughts, and blizzards. A multitude of men bore the name "Ole."

In 1893, the Great Northern Railroad, which began in St. Paul, Minnesota, reached Seattle, Washington. It was the only successful, privately-funded transcontinental railroad in the United States. A trip from Seattle to St. Paul took 69 hours and cost $35. Later the fare was reduced to $25.

Shanghaiing took place in Seattle in 1893. This was the practice of kidnapping men to serve as sailors. Laws at that time made it illegal for a man to leave a ship until the voyage was completed. Men were enslaved often through dishonest means and forced to sign on. Escape meant imprisonment. Not until the passing of laws between 1895 and 1915 did these practices finally end.

one

1893

"Wheatly! Catch that rope!"

Keane Wheatly jumped out of the way as the loose rope flying through the air narrowly missed his head. He watched for it to return and lunged for it. The roughness of the cord sliding through his hands no longer tore them apart as it once had. His callouses were thick enough, better than gloves at protecting his palms now. He grabbed and pulled the rope until it was taut and then efficiently tied it down. He worked as fast as he could with the gale winds trying to toss him overboard, then he fought his way to the door that would take him below deck.

The tossing of the ship no longer made him sick as it had the first few weeks on board. Now those weeks had turned into months and those months into years with no end in sight. Somehow he had to get off this ship and back to his family.

"Wheatly! That rope should have been tied down well enough to stand up to the wind!"

Keane held onto the rail and gritted his teeth as he waited for the first mate to approach him. The tall, red-faced man spat out his words in anger as he came nose-to-nose with Keane. The first mate wasn't much older than he was, but the whip in his hand and the burly man always at his side gave him an authority that Keane was forced to acknowledge. *Thor* was what the crew called the first mate, short for Thorpe. The dark, wavy hair could have made the man handsome, but the inner evil in him turned his features into nothing less than monstrous. And even though he could have had the bosun give orders to Keane, Thor seemed to relish having control over Keane himself.

"A mistake like that could cost us the ship! I ought to give you a taste of the cat 'o nines for such a stupid blunder! You watch yourself or you'll find yourself back in irons."

Keane kept control of his features as Thor ranted on until the first mate finally pushed his way past Keane. It had taken time and temper control to finally learn how to live with his present situation, but he was afraid every day of finally being pushed beyond his breaking point.

His grip on the ropes tightened as the dark, black waves tossed the ship. The crests broke into white spray over and over, some attacking him and trying to sweep him back into the ocean with them. There had been times he wanted to let them, to let go and let the ocean take him away from his prison. But he endured with the hope that someday he would find a way to escape.

This should never have happened to him.

A shiver ran down his spine as the same fears he had envisioned time and time again ran through his mind. His parents were getting on in years and having him disappear the way he did must have caused them no end of worry. Most likely they believed him dead by now. But of greater concern to him was that they could be dead before he ever found a way to return to them.

He shook away his fears as he made his way down the steps and to the galley. The ship creaked and groaned as it rolled about in the sea, but he paid it no mind. In his early days on board he had wished the ship would actually sink and take him down with it. Now all he wanted was to find a way to survive so he could get off it and back to the land and family he missed so much.

Keane grabbed the dish the cook handed him and slid onto the bench next to the man they all referred to as Preacher and began eating the unappetizing meal with haste. There was no loitering allowed in the galley as there were always others waiting a turn for their meal. Preacher also ate in haste, but he took time to nod a greeting to Keane, and even that small gesture cheered the distraught man somewhat.

More backbreaking labor ate up the hours until he could finally hit his bunk. Keane almost preferred the work to the sleep because his thoughts tortured him when he was finally at rest. Tonight he was surprised to see Preacher sitting on the bunk across from his when he entered the quarters he shared with several others.

Talking among the men was restricted by the captain as he didn't want them getting together and planning a mutiny was Keane's guess. But the captain's men couldn't be everywhere, and the men did talk. Keane sat down and pulled off his boots before stretching out on the bunk. He knew that Preacher was sitting there watching him like he had something to say. Keane was in no mood for a sermon, but Preacher's opening words caught him off guard.

"We need to get off this ship."

Keane's eyes flew open. He turned his head to study the thin, muscled man beside him. "I thought you would be a man of peace, Preacher. How could we escape without bloodshed?"

Preacher's grin was almost hidden under the shaggy, brown beard on his face. "I'm not against sending a man to meet his Maker. It's only the ones who haven't met him before their demise who need to worry about it."

Keane glanced toward the passageway door and lowered his voice. "Have you a plan in mind?"

Preacher unfolded his long frame onto the bunk and whispered, "A rough one at best. We'll talk again." His eyes shut just as Keane heard a scrape of a boot outside the door. He, too, closed his eyes and feigned sleep as the jacktar made his rounds.

Keane's mind worked while his body rested. How could they possibly gain control? The captain had a lot of men working for him whose only jobs were to keep the shanghaied men at work sailing the ship. They did none of the rigging or deck work themselves. They guarded and kept control of the men's every movement. When they stopped at a port, the men were even more strictly guarded and not allowed on deck unless they were required for loading cargo. Often they were put in irons during port calls to keep them from escaping and more than once new men had been brought on the ship, shanghaied just as Keane had been in Seattle nearly a year ago.

Keane heard Preacher's even breathing and knew there would be no more talk tonight. He allowed his thoughts to go back to that fateful day when his life and freedom were taken from him.

He told his parents that he would go find work away from the farm to help them get through the lean times they were experiencing. Crops were poor due to the severe weather of previous years, and he just knew that if he could land a good job with the railroad, he could send money to help his family get by until the next season. Tears stung at his eyelids as he relived those last days with his family. His mother had sorrow in her face every time he looked at her, but she showed her love for him in the dishes she prepared before his departure. His father hid his emotion behind a mask of sternness, but Keane recalled seeing the quiver of his father's lips as he bade them good-bye.

It took time to get established on a railroad crew and the work was hard, but Keane was eager to earn some money, so he was willing to do whatever task was assigned him. It also gave him the opportunity to travel across the country and see things a farm boy from Minnesota would never be able to see had he stayed at the farm. His time working on the Great Northern Railroad opened his eyes to lands he had never envisioned, mountains he had only read about, and finally to an ocean which stretched beyond his physical sight.

He enjoyed some of it. There were times he forgot about the dear ones waiting at home for word from him and he joined his new buddies and spent some of his hard-earned money on pleasures for himself.

He moved on with the railroad, and he didn't care where it took him. When he realized that he had traveled and worked his way to the west coast, he seemed to wake up and look about him. Men were lined up hoping for a chance at a job with the railroad, just as he had done. He saw their haggard, desperate faces and remembered that he had parents who were counting on him to help them. He could not afford to lose his job to another.

But the railroad crew went to a tavern that night, and Keane joined them. He wasn't much of a drinking man, but he wasn't against it either. As the men about him drank and reveled the night away, he found a corner and took out paper and pencil and began a letter to home. He needed to send money to his folks and quickly. He had to find a way to get it to them. He was just folding his letter when a man stumbled into his table, nearly upsetting it.

"C'mon, Wheatly! Ya ain't drinkin' yer share!" It was one of the men from the Seattle crew, who stood, swaying and waving a pint of brew in his face. "This one's on me, pal. Drink up!"

Keane rescued the mug just as the man was about to fall onto his lap. He pushed the railroad man to his feet and raised the mug to him. "Thanks, friend. Hey, Smitty!" he called to one of his co-workers.

The man named Smitty was tall and lean and had his hat pulled low over his eyes. He walked to Keane's table with a scowl on his face.

"Let's get outta here, Keane. I don't like this crowd, I don't like the stink of the bay, and I don't care for the taste of their brew." Smitty was recognized as the complainer of the crew. Nothing suited him—ever. Even on the rare days when everything was going smoothly, he found the fly in the honey.

But this time Keane agreed with him. "I'll be out in a minute after I finish my mug. But, here, Smitty, I want you to do something for me. Your writing is better than mine. Would you put the address on this envelope to my folks for me? This here's what I need you to write." He pulled another piece of paper from a pocket and handed both it and the envelope of money to the man.

Smitty squinted his eyes to read the paper. "I can't see to read this in here. Too dark. I'll do it back at the site. You comin'?" He pocketed the paper and envelope and turned for the door.

"I'll be right behind you." Keane swigged at the mug and started to rise. He could see Smitty shoulder his way through the sea of men and he started after him, but the men all seemed to close in around him and even though he tried pushing his way through, he didn't seem to have the strength to make the men move. The room was growing darker and the door was farther away than he thought. He saw Smitty's head above the other men's and he tried calling to him, but no sound came from his mouth.

The next thing he knew, he was waking up in the hold of a ship, irons clamped about his ankles, the stink of fish in his nostrils, and the nausea of seasickness in his belly. He had been shanghaied. The man in the tavern gave him a spiked brew, and once he was drugged, he was hauled to the ship along with the other victims of the day. Even though it happened so long ago, Keane felt as if a lifetime had passed—his lifetime.

Those first days were the darkest of his life. Being shackled like an animal, beaten, whipped, and deprived of food, he finally succumbed and began doing the work he was being forced to do. It was actually Preacher's example that turned him around more than anything else. The man, shanghaied like the rest of them, did his work and then some. He never argued, never talked back, and when asked by one of the other prisoners why, he quietly and calmly answered, "If I'm ever going to get home again, I need to be in one piece."

Several days went by since Keane's short talk with Preacher about escape. Ideas ran through his mind about what they could do, but nothing seemed plausible. His biggest fear since talking about it was that Preacher might have mentioned his plan to others and that word of it would somehow reach the captain or his men. He finally got his opportunity to speak to the man when they ended up sharing quarters again.

Preacher began without preamble as Keane removed his boots. "We will be coming back into port in a few weeks to unload. Now the way I see it—"

"Hold on, Preacher." Keane interrupted, being careful to keep his voice low. "Who else have you got roped into this scheme of yours?"

Preacher raised an eyebrow at the question. "You backing out already?"

Keane shook his head. "No one wants to get off this ship worse than I do, but jumping overboard has been tried before and you know what happened."

Preacher studied Keane's face then suddenly cocked his head. He made a quick motion to Keane and both of them dove into their bunks. This time it wasn't the guard checking on them, but rather more of the men who shared the same quarters. The men trudged in and dropped to their bunks without a word.

No more opportunity to talk. Keane tried to suppress his frustration. He glanced over at Preacher and was surprised to see the man give him a smile and a wink. Keane hesitated then gave him a quick nod. Preacher closed his eyes and Keane followed suit.

Does he have another plan in mind?

He couldn't help but tense as he recalled the two men who were fished out of the water and their punishment for trying to escape was to be keelhauled under the ship until they drowned, a persuasive example to anyone foolish enough to attempt it themselves. Keane tried to relax and let sleep overtake him, but his thoughts were drawn to his folks and what was happening to them. At moments like this he wished he knew something about God, some way to tell him about his needs, some way to ask him to take care of his family for him, but Keane didn't know much about God apart from singing some hymns in their small country church and daydreaming through the sermons. He didn't even know if God would think him worthy of being helped. He knew all too well his own unworthiness.

It was the next day atop deck that the Preacher worked his way over to Keane. The sea was calm, the sun hot, and the creaking and groaning of the wooden clipper ship muffled the words that only Keane heard him say.

"There's a way. It's nigh to impossible, my friend, but I'm a man of faith and with God all things are possible." He didn't look at Keane as he spoke, but rather kept his eyes on the horizon as his hands worked through the ropes he was coiling.

Keane looked out at the endless ocean. He had to move on to his next task, but as he passed Preacher he said, "You better hope your God is on our side."

Preacher quietly chuckled. "He is."

two

"Mrs. Wheatly, are you home?"

Mina knocked softly on the wooden-framed door, afraid to make too much noise in case Mr. Wheatly was napping. She moved the basket of goods she carried to her other arm and tried to peer through the small glass window in the door. She backed away when the door began to swing out to her.

"Yes? Oh, hello."

"Good morning, Mrs. Wheatly. Do you remember me? We met in town the other day. I'm Mina. Mina Prescott."

"Yes, yes, I remember. Do come in. Is there anything wrong, Miss Prescott?"

Mina stepped into what appeared to be an entryway where the Wheatlys hung their coats and left their outdoor shoes and barn boots. Everything was neatly arranged, she noted, as she followed the older woman through to the dining room. The floor sloped slightly under her feet as she crossed to a chair Mrs. Wheatly held out for her.

"Everything is just fine, Mrs. Wheatly. I'm sorry if this is a bad time, but you said you would show me how to make those delicious rolls you shared with me, and I wondered if today would work for you. See, I brought the ingredients you mentioned." Mina stood by the chair and set the heavy basket on the table. She began pulling out bags of flour and sugar, spices, butter, milk, and eggs. She pretended not to notice how the woman stared at the bounty before her.

"You want to make rolls?"

Mina's smile was genuine. "If you have time today. If not, perhaps I could come back and you could show me another time." She reached into the basket again and pulled out some jars. "Mother put up the most delicious strawberry jam last year when we were still in Ohio. I just know it will go with the rolls so nicely."

Mrs. Wheatly seemed to study the dark-haired, young girl standing in front of her before making up her mind. "I guess we would have time before Thane gets in from the fields. It takes him longer these days to do the work without Keane here to help." She looked at the goods on the table. "How many batches were you planning on making?"

Mina laughed. "Oh, just enough to learn how. Mother says she's done all she can to teach me, but for some reason I don't have the knack for working with dough." She picked up some of the items and began carrying them through to the kitchen as she talked. "My breads always come out so hard and dense and chewy, but that roll you gave me was so light and heavenly, I just had to learn how you do it." She stepped back to the table to get the rest of the ingredients, not giving Mrs. Wheatly an opportunity to refuse her. "Did I bring everything we need?"

"That and more." Mrs. Wheatly pulled down an apron from a hook and went to a drawer to get another for Mina. "Well, Miss Prescott, let's bake rolls."

Mina smiled to herself at her victory. "Call me Mina, please. And thank you ever so much for letting me barge in on you like this."

The women went to work with the older instructing the younger, and they soon had dough rising nicely in a covered bowl. Mrs. Wheatly poured some coffee into cups and motioned for the younger girl to take a seat at the table. Mina noted the streaks of gray in the woman's brown hair and the dark circles under her eyes. Everything in the small kitchen was spotless, evidence of the hard-working woman's labors.

"Now we rest while it does its work for us."

"You mean while it rises? It's supposed to rise now, right? Mine never does that properly."

"Maybe you don't have good sourdough starter. I'll send some home with you."

They sipped at their coffee and Mina was aware that the older woman was studying her again. Perhaps it was odd that she showed up, unannounced at their doorstep, but when Mina saw the older couple sharing a roll after they had given their only other one to her, she was instantly aware of their need. She only wished she had realized it before she had exclaimed how delicious the rolls looked and had been offered one. She hadn't known at the time that it was all they had with them.

Mina had enjoyed conversing with the Wheatlys that day and learning that their son was away but that they expected him to return soon. They mentioned him so many times in the short time she visited with them, that it made her curious and she asked her mother that evening what she knew of them. The Prescotts hadn't been in town very long, and were only temporarily running the Austinson and Asleson General Store while the owners were away. They were quickly learning about the people in the area.

"The Wheatlys? Oh, yes. I believe that like the other farmers in the area, they had a rough time last year. Their son went off to find work so he could send some money home to help them get through this time, but that was over a year ago, and the last they heard from him was a letter and some money when he was in Seattle, Washington. I do hope nothing happened to him."

"They look like they aren't getting enough to eat. Would it be okay if I checked on them occasionally?"

Her mother smiled at her. "Of course."

Mina's thoughts came back to the present when Mrs. Wheatly spoke.

"Mina is an unusual name."

Mina wrinkled her nose as she smiled at her hostess. "Well, it's not my real name, actually. My father wanted me named after his Grandmother Wilhelmina, but I've always been called just Mina."

"Oh my." Mrs. Wheatly's mouth opened into an *O*.

"What is it?"

The older woman smiled and a mischievous glint appeared in her eyes.

"Mrs. Wheatly?"

"Maybe you should call me by my name, dear. It's Helma, short for…"

"Oh my!"

"Yes, it's short for Wilhelmina."

They laughed together.

"I think that it is wonderful to share a name with you, Helma. An honor, in fact. Now if I can just acquire your skill as a baker."

They laughed again and soon returned to the making of the rolls. By the time the golden brown rolls were sampled and declared delicious, the two women had become friends. Mina packed a few of the rolls to take home to her parents to sample, but she insisted on leaving the rest for the Wheatly's evening meal. When Helma tried to return the unused ingredients to her basket, Mina deftly moved aside.

"No, use them here and I'll be back to learn more from you, if that is okay?"

The older woman made to protest keeping the food, but Mina said in her sweet way, "Please. It is little enough thanks if it means I can bake like you."

Helma cocked her head to one side. "I should refuse because I can be a proud and stubborn woman, but I am not a stupid woman. Thank you, Mina."

Impulsively, Mina reached out and hugged her new friend. "No. Thank *you*. May I come visit you again?"

"Of course, Mina. Come anytime."

Helma walked Mina to the door and opened it, but when the younger woman gasped, she looked past her and saw several Indians standing quietly in front of the house.

"It's all right, Mina. We get visits occasionally from our Indian friends. Helma stood in front of Mina and smiled a greeting. She exchanged some words with the callers then nodded and went back into the kitchen, leaving Mina staring wide-eyed at the men, some in buckskins, and some in the same work clothing as the men around the area. They stared back at her in silence.

Soon Helma was back with a sack of the freshly baked rolls which she handed to one of the men. They took the sack and left as quietly as they had appeared. Helma stepped out of the house and pointed to a small pile of fish the men left behind.

"I'm sorry to give away all your hard work, Mina, but the Indians love freshly baked bread. I bet they could smell it baking. Don't be frightened, dear. They wouldn't harm you, and they are always generous in bringing something like these fish or venison or wild turkeys."

Mina stepped outside and looked around. "Where did they go? How did they disappear so fast?"

Helma laughed softly. "I don't know."

Mina was deep in thought as she started the horse back to town. She looked out over the fields that were struggling to produce the crops so desperately needed by the farmers. Rain was slow in coming and the ground was dry, but according to the locals, it was not the first time they had seen this cycle. Many were optimistic that things would improve soon. Mina could only hope and pray they were right because people like the Wheatlys were finding it harder and harder to get by. It made her feel better to know that their Indian friends helped them out.

Helma talked a lot about their son Keane. The picture she showed Mina was of him as a schoolboy, standing relaxed for the photographer, yet Mina could see a seriousness in his expression that belied his years. Mina could hear worry in Helma's voice and turned aside when the woman had to wipe away her tears. Since money had arrived from Keane, that seemed to mean that he was working and trying to help out his parents, but over a year had gone by with no word from him and that could mean that something had happened. Mina prayed, for the sake of the older couple, that they would hear from their son again soon.

"Lord Jesus, I want to help. Show me how to do it without offending them. And if their son is out there somewhere, please bring him back soon. They need him."

Helma watched the young woman direct her horse and wagon down the long drive from the farmhouse. It was so thoughtful and kind of her to come, and as she turned back to her kitchen and viewed all the supplies left behind, she was grateful for the caring and generous attitude of her new friend. It went against the grain for Helma to take anything in charity, but she couldn't let her pride get in the way of her good sense.

If only Keane would return!

Helma knew things would right themselves once more if her son was there. He was such a good son and tried so hard to bring happiness to his older parents. She and Thane were in their forties when they married and had a son. Keane seemed more like a grandson to them, especially when they were in town among other families and the younger people who had children Keane's age. But Helma didn't mind. Her son was a blessing that she had thought never to experience and even though they raised him with discipline and gentle training, she heaped all the love she had on him, her one and only child.

Please come back to us, Keane. Let us see you one more time before we go to our graves.

three

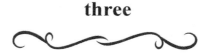

The days passed in a blur, a mixture of toiling, eating, and sleeping with no end in sight. There were times Keane thought he had only dreamed of Preacher's tantalizing hint of an escape. No more had been said and even though they passed each other as they went about their duties, there were no more winks nor even an acknowledgement that the man recognized him. A heavy weight of despair made every task more difficult than it had been before when there had been that inkling of hope.

"Wheatly! Get your mind on your job! Cap'n says there's a storm brewin'. Everything has to be battened down now. Move it!"

Keane gave the bosun a quick nod and began pulling in sails. He could see the first mate standing with his feet braced against the wind watching him. He felt the bite of the wind as it whipped at the hair he had tied at the nape of his neck. He glanced over his shoulder at the dark clouds advancing and felt a shiver of fear run down his spine. Months at sea still hadn't prepared him for the ferociousness of the storms they had encountered, and even though he felt he could no longer endure the life he was living, the thought of death in an angry sea frightened him even worse.

The ropes fought against Keane until another pair of hands joined with his and they managed to fasten the ropes down. Keane raised his head as Preacher shouted into his ear over the whine of the wind.

"This storm's a godsend. We have to go tonight."

Keane stared in disbelief at the man. "In this? You want to go overboard in this? It's a certain death, man!"

"Trust me. It's the only way." The preacher stared hard at Keane, and something in his expression told Keane he was right. He swallowed back the bile that rose with his fear.

"When?"

A brief closing of Preacher's eyes revealed his relief. "I'll get you." With that he moved off, clutching the side of the ship as it rode the swells.

Keane swung around as a hand grabbed his shoulder. Thor shouted words at him that the wind snatched away, but Keane understood his orders as the man pointed to barrels that were starting to roll around the deck. He grabbed a coil of rope and went to work to fasten them down.

He's crazy! We'll never live through the storm. What was Preacher thinking? Even with something to hang onto in this wild water, they'd eventually drown. Preacher thought they were coming into port, but how far was it? *We can't make it!* Yet, if he didn't try something, he was doomed to his imprisonment until death took him anyway.

Death. What would it be like?

Keane gasped as a barrel hit him in the side. The storm was gaining strength. He worked rapidly to get the cargo fastened down before heading to the hatch. The sky was dark, and white caps tossed the ship around as if it were a toy. He dropped the door to the hatch as water smashed onto it.

There was murmuring among the men who huddled in the galley. Some seemed to be praying, others stared blankly, disassociating themselves from their danger. Keane clung to a beam as the ship rose and fell and tipped and swayed. He searched for Preacher but couldn't spot him in the crowded room. The howl of the wind and a spray of salt water announced the first mate's presence as he and his man came down the ladder. Thor stood with his whip in his hand, water running from his clothing like he had just stepped from the sea, and searched the room until he found Keane.

"Rope's loose on those barrels, Wheatly! Get up there and do the job right."

Keane stared at Thor. The ropes couldn't have gotten loose, not the way he tied them. Was this the Preacher's doings?

"I said get up there!" Thor snapped his whip at Keane, but he ducked the blow. The man's eyes squinted as his mouth snarled into a hateful grin, and Keane knew full well that Thor enjoyed seeing his fear. Keane started for the ladder, crashing from side to side into the men standing about until he reached it. He took one last look at the others, some not willing to look up, knowing he may not return. It was akin to murder to send a man topside in what had to be hurricane conditions, but there was no help for it.

Two men were needed to help him lift the hatch, and he barely squeezed through it before it slammed shut on them. He lay on the deck, clinging to the ring handle of the hatch until he felt something smash into him. He grabbed onto an arm.

Preacher clutched Keane's shoulders and helped him to his feet. It was too dark to make out his face, but Keane caught some of the words shouted in his ear.

"...rowboat ready...got to...now!"

The rowboat? Is he serious?

Preacher didn't release his arm as they got to their knees and crawled along. Keane struggled beside him, fighting the wind and being banged from side to side as the waves tipped the ship. He didn't know how Preacher was able to get access to the boat, and he didn't believe they would survive in one, but he was committed now. Once the first mate ordered him back on deck, he knew he was being sent to his death. Preacher's scheme was his only hope.

He felt Preacher pull on his arm and he got to his feet.

"Over! Climb over!"

He heard the words, but couldn't see anything. He felt Preacher give him a push, and he scrambled to put his leg over the side, reaching into the darkness for something to jump into. For a moment Preacher let go of him, and Keane panicked and started to scramble back to the deck, but something grabbed his leg and pulled, and he reached out until his hand struck Preacher's head.

"Let go! Drop!"

Spikes of rain shot at Keane's eyes as he tried to see. He was soaked through as if he had already jumped into the sea and he couldn't maintain his grasp on Preacher's head. He slid off the side of the ship and for a moment he fell into nothingness and then he landed with a thud onto the bottom of the tiny lifeboat.

"Wait for the swell that tips the ship toward us!" yelled Preacher. "Then cut the rope."

Keane felt a knife pressed into his hand. He had only moments to wonder how the man had gotten his hands on a knife when he felt the wave coming. He scrambled to his feet. The small boat scraped along the side of the ship as the wave brought the ship down to the water's level. Keane swung his arm wildly, trying to find the rope and connected with it. He grabbed on and sliced at it with the knife. The boat lurched forward as Preacher cut through his side and Keane desperately hacked at the rope before it fell headlong into the water. It broke loose and they fell just as the ship bobbed away from them. Keane's head struck something as he fell into the boat again.

"Quick! We have to push off before the ship rolls back!"

Keane searched, pawing with his hands until he felt an oar, and he pushed it against the ship then began paddling to get the small boat away from the large one. He had no idea if he was paddling with or against Preacher's efforts.

"Keep it up, Man! It's working!"

Keane pulled the oar through the water with all the strength he had. He only stopped when the boat felt as it were about to capsize and he would grab onto the side and fight against the waves that tried to pull him away with them. Then he would paddle again until the next swell would threaten. Over and over he and Preacher fought the sea and clung to the boat. His muscles screamed in pain and he gasped for air, only to have his mouth fill with the salt water that continually swept over him. He was exhausted and exhilarated at the same time.

He was free.

Another wave crashed over the boat, and Keane became conscious of the fact that he was sitting almost waist high in water. He may be free of the ship, but he wasn't free from the ocean. Not yet.

"We'll sink if we don't get this water out of here!" he shouted, hoping Preacher could hear him above the storm.

"Okay...stabilizes...got to...keep going."

It was hard to hear the words shouted back to him, but he understood that they had to keep going. He grabbed onto the side as the boat tipped to a dangerous angle. Then he began paddling again.

Suddenly a crack of lightning blinded him and the thunder immediately following was deafening.

"Look!"

Keane swung around and some distance away he saw a light.

"What is that?" He shouted to Preacher.

He could see the outline of the man in the boat with him now, but he turned back to see where Preacher was pointing.

"It's fire. Lightning struck the ship."

"But how? How could anything burn? Everything must be soaked from this rain."

They both grabbed onto the side and rode out another wave that threatened to tip them.

"It's those barrels." Preacher moved closer to Keane. "I untied them so that Thor would send you back on top."

It was what Keane had suspected. He tried to make out Preacher's features, but he could only squint against the rain and wind.

"I knew he would make *you* go up there. One of them must have broken loose and spilled oil across the deck. Look at that!"

The ship was farther away now, but the distant light they had seen at first now blazed higher and higher.

"More barrels." Keane knew that even the barrels still tied down were no match for the ferocity of the storm. They must have all broken up and spilled out their cargo.

"All those men." Preacher's voice was solemn, but Keane heard him. Another swell made them grab on to the sides of their little boat and then the ship was lost to their sight.

four

Mina walked past the flourishing fields with thankfulness in her heart. The rains hadn't been plentiful, but they were sufficient to make a difference, and optimism was beginning to show in the faces of the people who came into town to shop at the store. She smiled as she thought of how much the success of the crops would mean to farmers like the Wheatlys.

It had only been a few months since the Prescotts moved to the rural community of Ulen. Mina's father, though a successful businessman in Toledo, longed for a simpler life, and with his wife's approval moved their small family to Minnesota and agreed to run the mercantile and dry goods shop in the owners' absence. Her father thought this would be a good way to see if they wanted to stay in this small community and maybe open a business of their own.

The relaxed atmosphere of the farmers and townspeople brought new life into her father, and Mina never regretted giving up city living for the slower pace of the town when she saw the happiness in her parents' faces each time they welcomed their new friends into the store. At twenty-two, many of her friends thought she should have stayed in the city where she would have more opportunity to find a husband, but Mina wasn't worried. She was content to be with her family and work with them. Her future was in the Lord's hands, and she certainly wasn't interested in searching for a husband. She was as happy in this small town as her parents were. She smiled as she recalled a conversation they had with Mr. Melbye when they first got to town. Her father had asked the postmaster how the town came to be.

"Well, the name of the town was Ulen to start with after Ole Ulen, our first settler," the man told them. "Then Ole Odneland became postmaster and the name got changed to Odneland until Ole Asleson platted out the town and changed it back to Ulen again after Ole Ulen."

"Ole seems to be a popular name around here, Mr. Melbye," her father had commented, hiding a grin.

"Sure is. By the way, just call me Ole," the man replied with a wink.

Mina and her folks often joked with each other about the Ole's of Ulen.

It was a beautiful day for a walk, and even though Mina could have hitched up the horse and wagon for the three-mile journey out to the Wheatly farm, she didn't have a heavy basket to carry today, so instead she opted for a walk in the sunshine. She hummed the hymn they had sung in church the day before, "When I Survey the Wondrous Cross," meditating on the words as she did so, all the while keeping her steps in time to the rhythm of the music. The last line of the song brought a furrow to her brow.

"Love so amazing, so divine, Demands my soul, my life, my all."

The preacher explained how God used the Law to deal with the nation of Israel, giving them commandments and making demands on them—obey and be blessed; disobey and be punished. But that all changed through the ministry God gave to the Apostle Paul and the explanation that Christ's death on the cross provided forgiveness to all who would believe. God now offers salvation to all—Jew and Gentile—by grace through faith in Jesus Christ, who died for their sins, was buried, and rose again.

Mina smiled. No more demanding from God, but rather today we obey out of love toward him. She nodded in silent agreement as she recalled the preacher pointing out that God does give us instructions to follow in his Word, but that grace allows us to respond freely, and that disobedience does not mean punishment because Christ took that punishment of sin away on the cross.

She understood the last line of the song better now. God's love demands a response, and she wanted to use her life to show her response of love for God.

"I say, Mina! Are you deaf? I've been calling your name!"

Mina turned with a start. So deep were her thoughts that she hadn't heard anyone coming up behind her. The young woman ran toward her with unladylike long strides and arrived red-faced, but not breathless at her side. Mina smiled in delight at being joined by Tuva Thomsen. Even though Tuva was three years younger than Mina, the two had become friends the first time they met, mainly due to Mina's outgoing personality. Tuva, with her braided-blonde hair was typical of many of the Scandinavians in the area—shy, reserved, not speaking unless spoken to— but Mina didn't let that stop her from peppering the young woman with questions until Tuva was forced to break out of her shell and respond. Still, it was only with Mina that Tuva opened up. Her reserve was still evident around others.

"I can't believe you couldn't hear me. I've been yelling for the last half mile!"

Mina laughed out loud. "You? I don't believe it." She linked arms with her friend. "Where are you headed?"

"I saw you walk out of town and thought you might be going to the Wheatlys again. Are you?"

Tuva waited for Mina's nod. "So I ran to the store to tell Mother I would go with you. By the time I got to the road, you were already way ahead."

"Well, I am very happy to have you join me." Mina threw her head back and her free arm out. "Isn't it a glorious day? Thank you, Lord!"

Tuva looked down at her friend, who only came as high as her shoulder. "You sure get excited about the sun shining."

Mina laughed at the expression on Tuva's face. "And why not? We have an amazing God and I want him to know how much I appreciate his creation."

Tuva was silent. As though reading her thoughts, Mina continued, "You feel the same, I know. You just tell him so in your own way, right?" She squeezed Tuva's arm.

"I do. I just figure he's not hard of hearing so there's no need to shout."

"Oh, Tuva! I love your sense of humor." Mina laughed. "I need to take lessons on decorum from you."

"Decorum? Did you see me running down the road like a race horse? Mother has practically given up on me being a lady, especially since you've come to town. She holds you up as an example of proper etiquette all the time. Could you please stumble once in a while or spill tea on someone at the Ladies' Aid Meeting? I can't measure up to you."

Mina was holding her hand over her mouth by this time to stifle her laughter while Tuva rambled on. It was most likely the longest speech ever to come out of her friend's mouth, and Mina enjoyed every word of it. "If you want to talk about measuring up, then you should know how much I envy you your tall, statuesque Norse goddess presence. Maybe I'm just loud to make up for being short."

The two walked along in silence for a while, then Mina shared with Tuva her thoughts on the sermon the previous day and the hymn that had been on her mind. "Sing it for me, Tuva. I wish you would sing out more in church. If I wasn't standing right beside you, I would never know how beautifully you sing."

"I'm not going to sing!" Tuva was incredulous at the request.

"Oh, come on. I'm the only one here. What better way to praise the Lord than to sing his praises out here in his creation?" Mina tried coaxing.

"Mina, you're impossible."

Mina knew it was of no use. It was one thing to get her friend to start talking, quite another to get her to sing out loud. But Mina knew she wouldn't give up trying. Tuva had a gift that should be shared.

The girls arrived at the Wheatly farm just as Thane Wheatly was finishing his lunch and heading out to the barn.

"I'll leave you hens to your visitin'," the older man joked. He thanked his wife for the meal and left the house with a smile back at the two visitors. "Good to see you, ladies."

Helma chuckled at her husband's remark, and Mina was glad to see some of the tension gone from her friend's face.

"Have you any word from your son?" Mina ventured as she helped set out cups while Helma put the coffee pot on but was immediately sorry she had mentioned him when worry creased Helma's face.

"No. Nothing. I'm afraid, Mina. I'm truly afraid that he's never coming back. We should have heard something by now. It's been almost two years now since his last letter." Helma pressed her fist to her mouth and her shoulders shook with silent sobs.

It was Tuva who gently took the woman by the arm and led her to a chair. "We've been praying for answers, Helma. God knows where Keane is and he's there with him. We've got to keep trusting him."

Mina was amazed. The words Tuva spoke came easily from her, and the look on her face as she comforted the older woman and talked about her son was akin to love. Was there something between Tuva and the Wheatly's son?

Mina quietly moved about the kitchen as the two spoke in muffled tones. She stopped to listen and heard Tuva say "Amen". They had prayed together! Mina was bursting with questions for Tuva, but held her tongue. Now was not the time. She carried the coffee pot to the table and set down the plate of cookies Helma had prepared.

"Thank you, Mina. And thank you, Tuva. You've always been a good friend to us." Helma brushed off her tears and straightened her hair. "Now we're going to focus on this good weather, the improvement in the crops, and have a nice visit. It is so good of you girls to come all this way out to see me."

It was some time later when the two girls were on their way back to town. They walked in silence, although Mina's thoughts were busy with questions she wanted to ask. Surprisingly, it was Tuva who broke the silence.

"You look like you're ready to pop, Mina."

The incongruous statement made Mina laugh out loud. She stopped and faced the taller girl.

"I thought I knew you pretty well, but...you..." She waved her hands in the air as if not knowing how to complete her thought.

Tuva's blonde head was down and her voice quiet. "Just because I don't talk a lot doesn't mean I don't know how."

"Oh, I know! It's just that...I mean...you seemed so comfortable..."

"The Wheatlys have been here as long as my family has, and Keane and I have grown up together. We all care about them."

Mina studied the lowered head. "And you care especially for Keane?"

Tuva didn't look at her friend as she answered. "No, nothing like that. I've actually never even spoken to Keane Wheatly. He was a couple years ahead of me in school."

Mina linked arms with Tuva and continued walking again.

"I see."

five

It was the longest, most exhausting night of Keane's life. Over and over he believed they would be tossed into the violent waves that rose and fell and crashed into their boat. The wind gusts seized the small craft and tried to flip it over when the waves failed to do so. The two men each pulled off a boot and frantically bailed water out even though it continually poured in. Keane wasn't even aware of the many times he cried out to God for help, but Preacher heard him. Each time Keane's boat mate would yell out words of encouragement to keep him going.

If the back-breaking work of a shanghaied sailor had any benefit to it at all, it at least served the men well in strengthening their bodies to endure the tortures of their fight with the sea. The storm abated as the morning light pushed the darkness away, and Keane lay back, waist high in water, trying to catch his breath while Preacher dipped boot after boot of water and dumped it over the side without looking up.

Keane forced his eyes open to look at the other man as he took up his boot and began bailing water again. Every muscle in his body screamed for relief as he dragged the boot through the swirling water in the boat and hoisted it with both hands to the edge to empty it. Then he did it again. And again. And again.

"Wheatly!"

Preacher's voice was hoarse and strained. Keane looked up and with effort turned his head to see where the other man was pointing.

"I knew we were coming to a port soon! It's land, man! Land! Get the oars. We have to get to it before we're carried back out to sea."

Keane felt a renewed energy take over his body. He fumbled with the oar but got ahold of it and plunged it into the sea and pulled with all his might. They paddled together as if in a canoe instead of the wide rowboat. Even though the oarlocks were there on the boat, the pins were gone from the oars. Once again Keane wondered how Preacher had gotten the boat and the oars and planned their escape.

The grayness of the morning light made shapes eerie, and distance was hard to judge. They could be miles from land, but no matter. It was there and even if it took their last ounce of energy, they were going to reach it. All conscious thought left Keane as he pulled and pulled and strained with all his might to make the small boat reach its goal. As if in a fog he heard Preacher's voice shout to him.

"We're going to come in fast. It's low tide now, which is good for us. We won't crash into those boulders, but we'll have to get out of this inlet as quickly as we can before high tide catches us. Are you up for some climbing?"

Keane's muscles shuddered under the strain of pulling the oar, but he yelled back to Preacher, "I'll make it."

A large wave gave them the final push to their destination. Preacher scrambled out the front of the boat and collapsed on the ground, but he hoisted himself up by pulling on the side of the rowboat and then tugging it with him as he tried to release it from the grasp of the sea. Keane stumbled toward the front of the boat to get out after him, but Preacher stopped him. His words came out in gasps.

"Get your...other boot...on first. The rocks and shells...are sharp."

Keane looked down at the blood flowing from Preacher's unbooted foot. He reached into the bottom of the boat and found the man's boot and handed it out to him while he emptied the water out of his and pulled it on. He was entirely soaked through, exhausted, and starved, but he was off that ship and on land again. He slid over the side of the boat and barely stayed upright as his legs hit solid ground.

Both men hung on to the boat for stability as they regained their breath and strength. Keane heard Preacher's hoarse voice.

"Thank you, Lord Jesus."

He put his arm around Preacher's shoulders. "Thank you, Preacher. Thank you for getting me out of there."

"We're not out yet." Preacher clasped Keane's arm. "But it's a start. First thing we have to do is sink this boat then get as far away from here as we can."

Keane shook his head. "But why?"

Preacher took another deep breath and coughed as he tried standing upright. "If crimps find it, they'll know someone escaped that ship."

"With the storm, won't they think men were escaping from a sinking ship?" Keane questioned.

"Can't take that chance. If they think that, they will be looking for the survivors. If none appear, they'll look for escapees."

Keane's heart sank. Will he never be free of the men who shanghaied him? He thought getting to land would be enough, but now Preacher was telling him they had to flee as quickly as they could. But how? They had no money.

He thought he had used up all his energy, but with the new fear of being caught again, he worked with Preacher to smash a hole in the boat with a sharp rock and push it out to sea again. The boat was already half-filled with water and didn't travel far before it disappeared under the surface. Then the men turned and faced the rocks around them.

Everything was wet and slimy, and they had to make their way slowly and carefully, climbing and slipping as they went. Fortunately it wasn't as steep as they feared and finally, chests heaving from the effort, they collapsed on grass, gripping it between their fingers for security.

Keane didn't know how long they lay there. He lifted his head and looked over at the man beside him. What a sight they must be! Their hair and beards hadn't seen a razor since being captured, their ragged clothing was barely sufficient to cover them, the swollen wet boots on their feet chafed their ankles raw. They were thin but hardened with muscle. The soaking from the storm was the first bath they'd had in a year. He shuddered to think of the diseases some of the men caught. Many died. But they were soon replaced.

"We better find shelter."

Keane nodded. It was daylight now. If they were spotted, questions would be raised. It would be better to stay hidden until they knew where they were and could decide what to do next. He pulled himself to his feet.

"Lead on, Preacher."

The man with him turned, and Keane could see a smile somewhere buried under his beard. "Name's Jake. Jake Rodwell. You got a first name, Wheatly?" He held out his hand as he introduced himself.

Keane's laugh was natural, which surprised him but made him realize that he was no longer under bondage. He hadn't heard his own laughter in how long? "Name's Keane. Good to know you, Jake."

They shook hands.

The sound of the crashing waves grew fainter as the two men moved away from the ocean. The trees began to multiply in number as they got further inland, and it wasn't long before they found a downed tree with brush grown up around it that served well as a resting place where they could be out of sight. Keane spotted some berries and tested them. They were sweet and plump, and he and Jake pulled them off the bushes and ate them until they could no longer stand. Then the men settled down among the brush and slept.

Jake opened his eyes but could see nothing. It was dark. He waited to feel the sway of the ship under him, but he wasn't moving. He heard the deep breathing of the man next to him, a hoot of an owl, the rustling of an animal through leaves, and then he remembered.

He was free.

A silent shudder went through him and he felt tears sting his eyes. So many times during their perilous night in the rowboat, he thought that would be the end. And if it had been, he would have welcomed it simply because he was off that dreaded ship. To die free of it was enough. But he was alive. Alive and free.

He made no move to get up. Not yet. He had to think about what to do next. He had to be careful, not only for himself, but also because young Keane was depending on him. Jake had spotted Keane when he was brought on the ship. He had seen his anger, his rebellion, and his outrage. He had felt all those things himself, and he had seen it in so many of the others. But Keane reminded him of himself. Like Jake, once Keane realized that the fight was fruitless, he settled down and endured, all the while planning an escape. Hope died out in so many of the others, but he could see hope hadn't dimmed in Keane's eyes any more than it had gone out in his own. That is why Jake approached him. He dared not risk his plan on someone who would not go into it wholeheartedly as Keane had done.

The night had been worse than he could have imagined, but they didn't quit. They made it. And they wouldn't quit now.

He heard Keane's breathing change and he waited until he heard him move.

"Ready to start walking again?" Jake whispered.

"You mean it wasn't a dream?"

Keane's words made Jake smile. One dream had come true. Maybe another would.

The men sat up. The heat of the day had dried much of their clothing, but they were still damp from lying on the ground, and their feet were swollen and sore from the wet boots. It would be difficult walking, but Keane had a solution.

"I've walked barefoot most of my life, I think I can get by."

"Not me." Jake winced as he started to pull a boot on. "Cut my foot pretty badly on those rocks."

"Let me see." Keane kneeled down and took the injured foot in his hand. "I'll tie what's left of my socks around it to protect it. You can tie yours around the other foot and we'll try that."

"You sure? You haven't gone barefoot in a while."

"It's better than those boots until they dry out."

Jake nodded his assent. There was enough of a moon to see their way through the trees, but he was unsure of which way to go. He checked the stars, knowing enough from being at sea to get his bearings and started them eastward. He knew they would have to find help somewhere, but where? As was his habit even before his ordeal at sea, he brought his requests to the Lord.

"What next, Lord? I know you aren't going to point the way, but I ask for wisdom to know what to do now. Thank you for getting us through the storm and sea. More than anything I want to be used of you to show others the way to heaven, especially Keane."

Jake stopped and held out an arm to stop Keane who was right behind him.

"What is it?"

Jake leaned close to Keane's ear. "A clearing up ahead. I think I see a cabin. Can you make it out?"

Keane peered through the darkness. "Yes, I think so. Should we go there?"

Jake searched the area around the building. "Let's wait until morning and see if there's any activity. We can rest here and keep watch."

As they settled down again, Jake heard Keane's stomach growl.

"Hope there's some food in there," his friend muttered in the darkness.

Jake smiled. He was glad that Keane didn't just barge ahead and try to find out if there was food. He was right in choosing him as a partner in his plan. Keane had learned the experience of patience. The verse from Romans came to Jake's mind, "And not only so, but we glory in tribulations also: knowing that tribulation worketh patience; And patience, experience; and experience, hope."

"And I have hope, Lord God. Hope that I will get home again, hope that I will find a future without Eva, and hope that Keane comes to you."

Jake was awake long before the sun made its appearance. He was carefully watching the cabin when Keane stirred, and he put a hand on the man's shoulder to keep him still. Keane turned his head to see where Jake was staring so intently and saw a woman come from the cabin and take a path to the out building in back. They waited to see if there was other activity in the cabin, but no one else appeared. Soon the woman was back and she went to the wood pile and gathered an armful of firewood before entering the cabin again.

"Think she's alone?"

Jake shrugged. "Seems like it, but I hate to frighten her by going up to the door, especially the way we look. Any ideas?"

Keane shook his head. A moment later he sniffed the air. "Do you smell that? She's frying bacon!"

Jake put his hand on the excited man's shoulder. "Could be she's fixing breakfast for someone other than herself. Let's see."

There was smoke coming from the chimney now, and the smell of food was tantalizing to the men. No one came out of the cabin for a time, then the woman appeared again carrying a wash tub. She wore a plain dark skirt, and the sleeves on her shirt were rolled up like she was ready to get to work. She went back in the cabin and returned with a bucket and headed to a pump in the yard.

"Seems she's alone. Let's try not to scare her, okay?" Jake stood and motioned for Keane to follow. He stopped when he was within sight of the woman and called out. "Ma'am! Please don't be frightened…"

The woman's reaction was so startling that Jake quit speaking mid-sentence. She took one look at the men and raced for the cabin, slamming the door behind her.

Jake swallowed and pulled at the tangled beard on his face. "Ma'am! We mean you no harm," he called out. He heard Keane's sharp intake of air when the door swung open again and the woman stood with a shotgun aimed at them.

"Go on! Get out of here! Get, I said!" The woman waved the gun menacingly.

The men stood very still, their hands held clear of their bodies to show they were hiding nothing. Jake tried again.

"Ma'am, I apologize that our appearance frightened you. We were in a boat in last night's storm. All we ask is a bit of food and maybe a way to get cleaned up. And could you tell us where we are? We need to find our families and let them know we are alive."

Jake's words seemed to get through to the woman. By now she had stepped a bit closer and the men could see she was probably in her fifties. Her gray hair was pulled tightly in a bun at the back of her head. Her frightened expression was changing to concern.

"Were you…were you shanghaied?"

Jake felt his shoulders relax in relief, but it was Keane who quickly answered.

"We were, Ma'am. We escaped last night. Could you please help us?"

The woman lowered her weapon and put a hand to her face. Jake saw she was holding back tears.

"My son." It was all she could manage to say.

Jake understood. "Your son was taken?"

She nodded. "It's been two years and not a word. He was…he was only fifteen. His name's Tom—Thomas Rogers. Have you seen him? Do you know anything about him?"

Keane drew in his breath sharply, but Jake put a hand on his arm. The two men who drowned, who were forcibly dragged under the ship at Thor's command, one was the kid.

"Mrs. Rogers, I—"

"He's dead, isn't he?"

Jake nodded. He saw Keane's hands ball into fists at his sides. Jake shook his head at him, feeling again the pain that had choked him when he could do nothing to stop the execution.

Mrs. Rogers dropped to the ground while sobs shook her.

"I'm sorry, Ma'am." Jake stopped Keane when the man would have stepped forward.

The woman wiped at her eyes and using the shotgun as a crutch to get back on her feet made an apology. "Forgive me."

The men murmured some words.

"I had hoped…" She wiped her face with her apron then sniffed and patted back her hair, straightening her shoulders as she surveyed the men before her. "You men need food. Come, I have breakfast cooking."

"Thank you, Ma'am. That would be most appreciated, but we cannot enter your home in our condition." Jake ducked his head as the woman stared at him, but he shrugged and pointed to his long hair and beard. "We can't risk passing the vermin growing in here on to you, Ma'am. And please forgive me for mentioning it."

Again Mrs. Rogers stared at the men. "You men have suffered a great deal. I can see that. I so wanted my Tommy back, but..." She paused and her next words were choked. "But God took him home. I will be thankful he is no longer suffering."

Jake felt his own tears and squeezed his eyes against them. His prayer was silent but heartfelt as he prayed for the woman in grief before him.

Mrs. Rogers cleared her throat. "I'm not about to let you men stand there starving because of some vermin. I'm heating water now to do the wash, but we'll use it instead to wash you. But, first, find a stump. I'll bring you out some food then we'll get started."

It seemed only moments when plates of hot food were placed in the men's hands. Keane was about to begin shoveling the food into his mouth, but he stopped when Jake bowed his head and gave thanks.

"Good thing you made that short, Preacher. I couldn't wait another second," he said around the food in his mouth.

"Preacher?"

Jake shrugged at Mrs. Rogers who had placed the question. "The men called me that, but I'm not a real preacher, Ma'am. I'm just a man who has been saved by the blood of Jesus. Name's Jake. Jake Rodwell. And this here's Keane Wheatly."

Keane nodded but kept on eating.

Mrs. Rogers watched them a moment. "I have so many questions for you, and when Mr. Rogers gets back from town, he'll want to know all you can tell us about Tommy, but let's take care of first things first."

She went back to the cabin, leaving the men to the food. Jake felt renewed strength from the nourishment but realized that he was full long before he wished to be finished eating. Keane was having the same trouble.

"I think our stomachs aren't used to such good food. We have to go easy, Keane."

In no time Mrs. Rogers was back, this time with a towel wrapped around her hair and a tray with razor, comb, scissors, and a mirror.

"I'll cut your hair first, Mr. Rodwell, while you get shaved, Mr. Wheatly. Then you can switch places."

"But we don't want you to have to touch…"

"Nonsense! You boys don't have anything that scares me. Now let's get this done so you can get baths."

Jake sat still, cringing while he felt the older woman clip clumps of ratted hair from his head. At least the torrential rains from the storm had washed him somewhat, but he could tell from her sighs and grunts that she was undaunted by the task. Keane stood in front of him shaved clean, and the white of his cheeks and chin was in stark contrast to the dark tan of the rest of him.

They switched places when Mrs. Rogers declared him done, and Jake stared at his reflection after he had removed the snarled beard from his face. He looked younger for having the beard gone, but so much older than he had before being shanghaied, so thin, so worn, yet toughened by his experience.

"If you would come here next, Mr. Rodwell?"

"Jake. Call me Jake, Mrs. Rogers. What is that you have there?"

"Kerosene."

Keane was coughing and sputtering as the woman doused his head with the liquid and scrubbed it into his shortened black hair.

"I suggest you use some while bathing as well, gentlemen. It will kill whatever vermin you might still have. The tub is set up around back of the house. I'll gather some clean clothes for you." With that Mrs. Rogers nodded for Jake to bend over while she scrubbed his head. "If you have no objection, I will burn the clothes you are wearing."

"Do you have—?" Jake sputtered and spit and coughed.

"Not a good time to be talking, Jake. Wait until I'm through."

Jake heard Keane chuckle, but he dared not say anything and kept his eyes tightly closed as he endured the hardest head scrubbing he'd ever had. Nothing could survive after Mrs. Rogers' treatment.

Keane took off for his bath while Jake ran the comb through his cropped hair. "I'm sorry to be such a bother to you, Ma'am, but Keane and I sure appreciate what you're doing for us. Can you tell me where we are?"

The woman kept busy scrubbing the pails she had just used while she answered. "We're north of Seattle about twelve miles or so."

Seattle! Jake's excitement must have shown on his face, for Mrs. Rogers stopped working to peer at him.

"Is that where you hoped to be, Jake? Are you from here?"

Jake nodded and took the buckets from the woman's hands and went to the pump to fill them. "I was shanghaied in Seattle three years ago."

"Three years!" Mrs. Rogers stared at Jake. "But you survived, thank God. Have you any family here?"

"No. Not anymore."

He dumped the water into the pot over the fire to prepare for his bath when Keane was done. He appreciated that Mrs. Rogers had stopped asking questions, but he felt he owed her an explanation.

"My wife died shortly before I was taken. There's no one here now, but I should still have a homestead, unless that's been taken from me too."

He felt her hand touch his back and he jerked away, startling the older woman, who backed away in alarm.

"I'm sorry, Ma'am. I didn't mean to frighten you. I'm just not used to...to..."

Mrs. Rogers' eyes filled with tears, but her voice was soothing and calming. "It's alright, son. No one's going to hurt you again."

Both men were scrubbed clean and hungry again in no time. Mrs. Rogers provided them with clothes that she said had belonged to her son.

"He was big for his age, my Tommy. I think he would be pleased to share them with you."

It was coming on to suppertime when they heard a wagon coming to the cabin. Jake pulled Keane into the shadows behind the cabin until they were sure that it was Mrs. Rogers' husband returning from his trip to town. The man's shoulders were stooped from years of hard work and his hands were gnarled and stiff, but gentle as he pulled his wife to him and let her sob out the story the two men had told her of their son. Jake watched the man close his eyes and bend his head to his wife's as they stood together in silence. Finally, Mrs. Rogers motioned for the men to come forward, and she made the introductions.

Jake shook Mr. Rogers' extended hand gently, afraid of hurting the knobby fingers, but the older man's grasp was strong, and he studied the two men carefully before speaking.

"You say your ship sunk?"

"We're not sure," Keane answered. "It was on fire from the oil barrels, I guess, but we couldn't tell what happened because of the storm and the waves and everything."

Jake watched Mr. Rogers stroke at the whisker nubs on his chin. "It didn't sink, boys."

Jake felt an icy chill go down his spine.

"That ship has caused a big stir in town. It took some bad blows from the storm, and it was burned and smashed up pretty good, but it made it."

Mr. Rogers paused to look at his wife. "I checked it out like I do all the ships, looking for Tom."

Mrs. Rogers nodded at her husband, her lips tightly closed.

"Usually I never get to see any of the crew, but men were jumping ship and swimming into port before anyone could stop them. Seems the captain and his men were all busy getting some injured and burnt people to shore to the doctor, and there wasn't much they could do about their crew escaping because of the damage to the ship."

Again he paused and looked at his wife. "I caught up with some of the ones escaping and found out about Tom." He squeezed her arm then he turned back to Jake and Keane. "Feller named Thorpe, the first mate, was badly burned in the fire, but not so badly that he couldn't holler about two seamen who abandoned the ship after starting it on fire. He claims he's going to find them two and see they are hanged for murder. Seems a couple of men drowned trying to get away from the fire."

"What? We never started that fire! It was lightning! It was—"

Jake put a hand on Keane's arm to stop him. "How badly was Thor—I mean Thorpe burnt?"

"Near's I could tell his left arm and side were what was wrong. Sounded like he got a blast of fire when he pushed open the hatch."

Jake took a deep breath. "They might not think we survived that storm in a rowboat." He looked at Keane. "The crimps will be out after the others who escaped too, and the law will back them up so they'll have help."

"The law?"

"Yes, Mrs. Rogers." Jake's voice was tired, but a note of bitterness crept in. "The law calls this desertion, even though we were taken against our will and our signatures were faked on the ship's articles. It means imprisonment or more likely, being put aboard another ship if we're caught."

"Now hold on," Mr. Rogers interrupted. "The government is working to put an end to that law. There's been a couple of laws passed...what were they called? The Maguire Act was one. It's meant to make it illegal to keep men on ship. There's another one too, but I can't remember what it's called. I've been trying to keep informed so we could help Tom..." He cleared his throat. "Anyway, it's not like it was."

Keane shook his head. "Thor won't let that stop him, Jake. Law or no law."

six

Thorpe heard the doctor moving from bedside to bedside, making his way closer to the hospital bed where he lay bandaged and suffering from his burns. He kept his eyes closed as the man reached his side and began his examination, but he didn't fool the physician.

"I'd say this was going to hurt me more than you, young man, but I know you won't believe that." The doctor gave orders to the nurse to begin peeling away the bandage and scraping the burned skin away. Thorpe tried to contain his pain from becoming audible, but he could not. Moans escaped through his tightly held lips.

"Let it out, man. There's no shame in admitting pain. I just wish I could relieve it better for you, but as this heals, we have to continue to remove the damaged areas to keep it from getting infected. Bear with us. We're doing our best to help you."

Thorpe made no reply. He steeled himself not to moan again, but beads of sweat rolled down his face as the nurse and doctor completed their task and placed a fresh bandage on his arm. Before they moved on, he felt a cold cloth mop his forehead, but he still refused to open his eyes. He heard them begin working on the next patient and he finally let himself release the breath he had been holding.

The pain from the burns was horrific, but nothing compared to the burning hatred inside him toward the two men he knew, *he knew,* had escaped the ship. Wheatly never returned from tying down the loose barrels. Sure, it was possible he had been swept overboard in the storm. Sending the man topside in the hurricane was cruel, but Thorpe had no sympathy for the enslaved sailors and cared little for their safety in any circumstance. But there was something about that Wheatly that always galled him. He had taken pleasure in breaking the man and making him obey his commands, yet there had always been that something in the man's face that told Thorpe that he hadn't broken his spirit as he had with so many others.

Wheatly hadn't returned. Thorpe gave the command for two of the men to open the hatch and look for him. He had to resort to the whip he kept by his side to get the men to obey. No one wanted to go topside. The men had all they could do to force the hatch open, and Thorpe had added his own strength by pushing against the door with his left arm. That's when the blazing oil had poured over him and down the hatch. He screamed as he hoisted his body out of the hatch and slid across the deck on his left side, soaking himself in spilled oil, which lit on fire. He scrambled out of his slicker while trying to keep from going overboard as the ship tipped on its side, only the fiery oil had gone down his sleeve and his arm continued to burn. He slapped at it and tried to smother it, but it burnt deep into his skin. His only relief were the sheets of rain that finally managed to wash the oil off the arm and finally off the deck. He was aware of men screaming as their bodies were burning. Some slid overboard. Maybe they jumped, he couldn't tell. They were doing anything to get away from the fire.

It wasn't until morning that the ship limped into Seattle's harbor. More men were jumping ship as land came into view and the crew were too busy handling their own wounded to stop them. Thorpe was unconscious by this time, but he heard reports from some of his men later about what had happened.

It was hearing that one of the lifeboats had been cut loose that convinced him that Wheatly had escaped. He didn't know for sure who else might have gone with him, but he guessed it might have been the man they called the Preacher. He was another one who hadn't displayed the crushed will of the others.

"They couldn't have survived, Thor."

That was the answer he got when he made his claims to the captain. "No one could have survived in those gale winds. Not in a rowboat."

"How could they have gotten to the boat?" was the question put by another seaman. The lifeboats were for the captain and his crew only. No provision was made for the shanghaied men should the ship sink. Two men were on guard at all times to keep any escapee from attempting to use the boats. But there were no men willing to be topside during the storm. Another reason Wheatly had to have used a lifeboat.

Thorpe knew the man had tried to escape. Was he alive? Did he survive? Was there another with him? The crimps would be rounding up the others who had jumped ship, but as soon as he could get out of the hospital, Thorpe determined that he was going to find Wheatly. He was going to find him and when he did, he was going to break the last spark of spirit in the man.

Keane was slowly beginning to feel like a human being again. Over a year of being beaten and treated like an animal had taken its toll, but having tasted freedom again, he felt hope. He looked at Jake and saw the change in him as well. He stood straighter, taller. There was a smile on his face as if he could not keep his joy to himself. Jake turned to him and spoke and his words told Keane that even though they had hope, they still weren't completely free.

"We can't stay in this area, Keane. The crimps are going to be looking for the men who escaped the ship, and they will especially be looking for us. By now, since the ship survived the storm and the fire, they will have found the cut ropes of the life boat and will suspect we took it."

"How will they know we made it to shore? That storm—"

"They won't know, but they'll do a search. I know how they work, how they think. I've been here long enough to see their dirty dealings and watch how they get the law to back them." Jake paused and scratched at his cleanly shaved chin. "My wife and I were going to leave the area but then she got sick and...and we couldn't leave. When she died, I wandered around like a lost man and didn't care what happened to me. I should have been more aware, more alert, but...Well, it's been three years. I need to find out what happened to my homestead. I had some money in the bank..."

Keane hesitated about interrupting the man's thoughts, but he knew decisions had to be made. "Couldn't you come to Minnesota with me? My folks would welcome you and we could sure use the help on the farm. I mean, until you know where you want to go. Anyway, they won't follow us all the way to Minnesota, will they?"

"No, of course not. But we can't let them know we made it out of that storm alive, just in case. We have to disappear as quickly as we can, but we'll need money. That's why I have to go into town to the bank and see if I still have some."

Keane studied his friend's face. "But it's too risky."

"It's got to be done."

It was decided that Jake and Mrs. Rogers would travel to town together. It was Mr. Rogers' suggestion that having a woman along would divert any suspicion that a man alone might bring on himself.

Jake was unsure what the outcome would be of his visit to the bank, and he expressed his concerns to the woman beside him on the wagon.

"I have no way to prove who I am. There were some bank papers we kept at our house, but by now they would surely be gone. In fact, I suspect that someone has moved in, perhaps found the paperwork, and has claimed my homestead and my money."

"Yes, that could be, but you won't know for sure until we check." Mrs. Rogers patted the younger man on the arm. "You have a good head on your shoulders, Jake. Let's just take this as it comes and not borrow more trouble."

It was two hours later that Jake pulled on the reins and pointed. "That's the place. Looks like someone is living there, alright."

The small field near the house was boasting a fine crop of wheat. The garden plot was neatly arranged in rows of vegetables, and a child played near the door of the house. Jake willed himself to remain calm. Seeing the child made his heart ache for the dreams he and Eva had of having a family. Everything was a picture of what he had hoped to achieve on the small homestead, yet someone else was there living his dream. He felt again Mrs. Rogers' hand on his arm and nodded to her in thanks for her sympathy.

They directed the wagon to the house where the child, a young boy, stopped his play and ran to the door calling for his mother. A young woman came out, pulling the boy into her arms. Jake saw that she was expecting another child. He felt an urge to drive on without approaching the woman. How could he tell her that she was living on his property?

The woman waited, shielding her eyes against the sun to see who had arrived. Jake was sure that having Mrs. Rogers at his side made him appear as less of a threat to the woman than had he been alone. She set the boy down and stepped forward.

"Yes, may I help you?"

Jake climbed down and helped Mrs. Rogers to descend while he tried to formulate the words in his mind he wished to say. Just then a man rounded one of the outbuildings and headed their way. No wonder the woman wasn't intimidated by the newcomers. Her husband was right there.

Jake waited for the man to reach them then held out his hand. "Good afternoon, sir. My name's Jake Rodwell and this here is Mrs. Rogers."

The man took his hand, but as soon as Jake said his name the woman gave a little gasp and the man stared hard at Jake.

"What did you say your name was?"

"Jacob Rodwell, sir." Jake waited while he watched the couple look at each other.

"I guess you're wondering what we're doing on your land, Mr. Rodwell."

The statement dumbfounded Jake. He hadn't expected a ready admission.

The man continued. "My name's Dorkin. Percy Dorkin. And this here's my wife Mathea. We came across this place nigh onto two years ago and since it was empty and we needed a place, we moved in. Now, I know it wasn't right of us to do so, mister, but like I said, we needed a place. My son here was about to be born and—"

"Looks like you've done a good job caring for it."

"Oh, we have, sir." Mathea Dorkin stepped forward. "We've tried our best to keep it up, but we always knew one day you'd come and want it back. Didn't we, Percy? We always said that when Mr. Rodwell came back, we'd move on."

"You thought I'd be back?" Jake was still unnerved by the couple's words.

"Yes, you see we found the graves out back." Mathea lowered her head as she said the words. "We're very sorry for your loss, sir. We've kept your wife and your son's graves as neat and tidy as we could for you."

Jake swallowed hard and tried to avoid Mrs. Rogers' questioning glance. He had told no one of the baby. Eva and the child had died within hours of each other.

"We'll pack up and be out of here as quickly as we can, sir. We hope you are not angry with us for using your lovely little home."

With difficulty Jake put aside the emotions he was feeling at the memories the couple had invoked in him. Clearing his throat, he managed to say, "No, there's no need for you to go."

The couple stared at him, not understanding.

"I...I would like you to stay. The place is yours. I just need to know if you found any paperwork inside. You see, it was in—"

"You mean it? We can stay here? We'll pay you, sir. We don't have much, but we'll pay for the place. Are you sure?"

Jake took a deep breath. "Yes, I'm sure. I think…Eva would have liked to have a family here."

Mathea could hardly contain herself. "Oh! We had so hoped to be able to stay. We love it here and the children…" She patted her enlarged abdomen. "Oh, Percy! It's like a miracle!"

Jake was unprepared for Mathea's hug, and Percy pumped his arm up and down thanking him over and over. Finally, Jake was able to speak again.

"I wonder if you found some papers."

"Oh, yes, Mr. Rodwell. Please forgive our excitement. It is how we knew your name. Your papers were there in the house in the desk just where you left them. We have kept it just as you had it, sir. If you would care to come in?"

"No."

Everyone stopped abruptly at his terse reply. "No, I would rather not, if you don't mind. If you could just get them for me."

Mrs. Rogers hadn't said a word up to this point, but before the awkward silence could continue, she knelt to eye-level with the little boy and began talking to him. The Dorkins went inside and returned quickly with the envelope of papers in their hands. Jake saw immediately that they were as he had left them. He scanned a few papers and looked at the Dorkins in amazement.

"You could have claimed these, and no one would have doubted you."

"I admit, sir, that we did move onto your land and into your home, but we always planned to move on once you came back. We were just sort of caretakers for you. But we would never steal from you or anyone."

Jake nodded thoughtfully. "You are good people. I can't thank you enough for protecting these papers for me. I was...called away unexpectedly and could only now return. Have you ink and pen? I would like to sign the land over to you and make it legal."

Mathea hurried back into the house. Jake pulled out the necessary papers and once he had the writing utensils, he signed and dated the document giving the Dorkins the right to own the property.

"That should do it." He brushed off their thanks again and turned to Mrs. Rogers. "If you wouldn't mind giving me a moment or two?"

She nodded her head in understanding. Tipping his hat at Mathea, Jake walked by them.

"He's going to the graves," Mathea whispered to her husband.

It was a quiet trip the rest of the way into the busy seaport town of Seattle. Jake was weary from the emotions he experienced as he stood beside the graves of his beloved wife and child, but he had to be in control to face any questions which may come his way at the bank. Mrs. Rogers offered the comfort he so badly needed.

"How old are you, Jake?"

The question puzzled him. "Thirty, I guess. I feel a lot older."

"You've endured more in your thirty years than most people will have to in their lifetimes." Mrs. Rogers patted his arm. "Those people look to be good folks. You handed them a treasure back there."

"I wonder where they would have moved on to."

"Didn't seem as if they had much, but they would have found something. No, you gave them a start that not many young people get these days. God bless you, Jacob."

The officer at the bank was vaguely familiar to Jake. Mrs. Rogers walked in with him and then stepped aside as he spoke with the man.

"Ah, yes, Mr. Rodwell. It has been a long time since you've come in. You have your papers with you, I see. What can I do for you?"

Relief flooded through Jake, but he kept his features under control. "I'd like to withdraw my funds, please."

"Yes, of course. You will see that there is some interest since you were here last. Goodness! By my calculations that was about three years ago. I will take care of this for you right away."

It didn't take long to do the transaction. Jake informed the officer of the new owners of his property and was about to leave when the man stopped him. The man had been all business before, but now there seemed to be a nervousness about him, and he lowered his voice as he spoke to Jake without making eye contact.

"Mr. Rodwell, I suggest that you leave town as quickly and as discreetly as possible."

Jake's hands stilled and he was on alert as the man continued.

"Inquiries have been made and your name mentioned, so you see, I fully expected you to come in at some point. But fear not, I do not answer to those hoodlums from the docks. You have been a good and faithful customer and I wish you well, but it is imperative that you disappear from here."

Jake's only answer was a quick nod. He motioned to Mrs. Rogers and took her arm. Together they exited the door, and Jake helped the older woman onto the wagon seat. He climbed up beside her and started the horse, keeping his actions as casual and controlled as possible, all the while wanting to flap the reins and set the horse at a gallop. He saw a man leaning against a building across the street and tried not to stare. He turned his head slightly away as the wagon went by. It was a crimp, he was sure of it. The man had all the earmarks of being one of the men who hunted down and shanghaied unsuspecting victims, imprisoning them on ships. The man only gave them a passing glance. Perhaps being with Mrs. Rogers had again saved him that day.

Once they were away from the town, Jake put the horse to a faster pace. He saw Mrs. Rogers' questioning glance, but kept on until he knew the horse needed a rest. He was about to explain when she questioned him.

"There was trouble then? Did the man threaten you?"

Jake took a deep breath. "Quite the contrary. He warned me. I expected all kinds of questions about me withdrawing my funds, but it was as if he was expecting me and had it all prepared ahead of time. He told me to leave quickly because men had been questioning him. Men from the docks."

"I see."

"I fear for you and your husband now. If they come looking, they may remember you being at the bank with me."

Mrs. Rogers adjusted her hat. "If they come looking, they'll get what they deserve. No, you and Keane are not to worry about us. They will get no information about you from us."

"That is not what I'm worried about."

"They are the ones who should be worried. With the new laws finally being passed, we may just bring them up on murder charges." Her voice broke, but she continued. "And your name never has to come into it. We have the word of others now to bring to the law. They are going to have to answer for their crimes. You mark my words."

Keane was eager to hear all that happened, but Jake forestalled his questions. "We have to leave now, tonight."

"You'll come with me then? To Minnesota?"

"Yes, if you'll have me along. I have to start over somewhere, and that's about as far from an ocean as we can get."

Mr. Rogers insisted that they take one of his horses. "You can leave it with a friend of mine. See, there's a spur off the tracks where the train takes on water. That would be a good spot for you to get on, and my friend's house is about a mile from there. Just put the horse in his stable and I'll be by in a few days to pick it up. He won't ask any questions."

Jake shook his head. "But I have money for tickets. We can board the train at a regular stop. No need for us to sneak on."

Mr. Rogers watched as his wife prepared some food for the two men. "I've been thinking on this. Don't you think they will have men watching the depots? You can pay the conductor once you're aboard, but I think you should still stay out of sight, just in case there's someone riding the train, you know?"

The men discussed the possibilities until Mrs. Rogers finished her preparations. Jake and Keane rose to take their leave of the kindly couple with reluctance. It was Mrs. Rogers who gave them the impetus they needed.

"Go. Get to safety and live the life my Tommy couldn't have. God be with you."

seven

Mina finished pinning her shiny, black hair and stepped over to the window. It was a gloriously sunny day, and people were out and about enjoying the nice weather. Today was the Ladies' Aid meeting, something Mina at first had balked at attending, but later when she found that other young ladies made it a habit to join their mothers, had gladly gone along. As with her baking, sewing skills were not among her accomplishments, but she was willing to learn. Most of all, she enjoyed the time to visit with her new friends, share in the refreshments, and listen to the Bible lesson. The women relied on Mrs. Evans to deliver the devotional for the summer, and a new speaker would be chosen for the next season.

"Mother, are you ready to go?" Mina called as she descended the staircase from the family's living quarters to the store below. "Oh, excuse me, Father, I didn't know you had a customer." Mina nodded politely to the farmer doing business at the counter. She pulled back the curtain covering the doorway to the storeroom and found her mother busily unpacking a crate.

"Mother, it's almost time to go. Can I finish that so you can get ready?"

Mrs. Prescott pushed back her hair. "I was hoping you'd say that. Goodness, the morning is flying by! I only need to touch up my hair and I'll be down. Just put these cans on the shelf and I'll tend to the rest when we get back."

Mina quickly stacked the cans of baking powder and tidied up the overflowing storeroom. Crocks of pickles, sacks of flour, sugar, rice, and oatmeal, rounds of cheese, and bags of candy were all neatly piled onto the shelves. A variety of spices gave the room a mysterious aroma that kept one guessing to identify each one. Mina twirled slowly in the crowded room, her eyes shut, as she breathed in deeply the enticing smells.

"Wilhelmina! What are you doing?"

Mina swirled around. "Oh, Father! You startled me." Her sheepish grin made her father laugh.

"Your mother is waiting out front for you." He kissed her forehead. "Have a good time, dear, and try keeping your eyes open."

Mina slipped past her father and joined her mother. Together they walked past the Ulen Union Office where Mina caught a glimpse of Mr. Reiersgord hard at work at his desk. She recalled that his first name, like so many of the townspeople, was Ole, and she was about to make a remark to her mother about it when her mother stopped suddenly causing Mina to bump into her.

"My word!"

"What's wrong, Mother?" Mina was busy straightening her hat which had been knocked askew by the collision. She glanced up and stared where her mother was pointing. "Why...why is there a house in the middle of the street?"

"Uh, well, I have no idea, but I'm sure the ladies at the Aid meeting will know. Come along or we'll be late."

The ladies were still greeting one another when the Prescotts arrived, and it wasn't long before Mina was seated beside Tuva. Tuva's mother was quick to bring up the unusual happening in town.

"I don't know what the feller thinks he's going to accomplish. It's the craziest stunt I've ever seen. Claims he's fed up paying taxes on his property, so he put wheels under his house and moved it to the street. Said he's already paid taxes to have the street built, so that's where he's going to live. Bet the Union will have the whole story."

Mina looked wide-eyed at Tuva who gave her a quick cross-eyed look back. Mina had to struggle to keep her giggles to herself, but her silent laughter made her prick her finger with the sewing needle. Tuva's expression when she said "ouch!" only made her laugh more.

But the big news of the day was that the Wheatlys had received a telegram from Seattle, Washington.

"It has to be word about that son of theirs. He took off, saying he was going to work and send them money, but I have it on the word of someone at the bank that he sent very little money. I figure he's been out gallivanting instead of remembering his folks back here struggling to get by. Young kids these days have no—"

The gossiping woman's outburst was cut short when Mrs. Evans stood with her open Bible in her hands. "Let's begin, shall we?" Though she never looked at the woman who had been speaking, there was a silent reprimand in the pursed lips of the lady who began the Bible study. Mina barely heard the reading of the Scripture passage as she wondered what the telegram could mean for the Wheatlys. Was it good news? Was their son coming home? Or did the message contain the sad news that he had died? She felt her mother nudge her arm and realized that her inattention was noticed. She gave her mother a brief nod and concentrated on what Mrs. Evans was saying.

"The Bible isn't a book of magic potions where we open it at random and point to a verse and think that is what God's instructions are for us for that day. II Timothy 2, verse 15, tells us to study the Word. We have to read verses in their contexts to get the full meaning of them. We have to know to whom God is speaking. Is it to the nation of Israel regarding prophecy yet to be fulfilled? Or is it to us, those of us who believe in Jesus Christ's death for our sins, his burial, and his resurrection for our salvation? We, who are known as the 'Body of Christ'? Does it pertain to our lives today or to a time to come?

"In Galatians, Paul warns the believers. He says, 'I marvel that ye are so soon removed from him that called you into the grace of Christ unto another gospel: Which is not another; but there be some that trouble you, and would pervert the gospel of Christ. But though we, or an angel from heaven, preach any other gospel unto you than that which we have preached unto you, let him be accursed. As we said before, so say I now again, If any man preach any other gospel unto you than that ye have received, let him be accursed.'

"We must handle God's Word correctly. I Timothy 4:13 says to 'give attendance to reading'. We need to be like the Bereans in Acts 17, who 'received the word with all readiness of mind, and searched the Scriptures daily, whether those things were so.'"

As Mrs. Evans closed out the devotional with prayer and the women began to partake of the refreshments, Mina felt convicted by the words she had heard. She knew she didn't read her Bible with a mind to study it. She read out of habit and sometimes just to get through a passage to say that she had done so. She listened in church, but she never felt the need to compare what she heard with the actual Scripture it came from to see if it was true. Part of the reason was that she was lazy, but in her heart she knew there was a desire to know God better and to know his Word better. She rose from her seat and approached the woman who had given the thought-provoking lesson.

She thought her quiet words of thanks were only heard by Mrs. Evans, but she felt her arm squeezed and turned to find her mother smiling at her with a glimmer of tears in her eyes. She smiled back in understanding.

Mina joined Tuva, who was balancing her plate of food in one arm and her baby brother in the other. A toddler was pressed against her knee trying to reach for the food on her plate.

"Goodness, Tuva, let me help." Mina set her plate aside and reached for the toddler.

"Sometimes I envy you being an only child, Mina." Tuva's words were emphasized with a longsuffering sigh.

Mina handed the toddler a cookie from her plate and tried to keep the boy's swinging legs from smacking her in the shin. "Oh, I'm not an only child, although I feel like one. I have an older brother. Didn't I tell you?"

"No. You do? Where is he?"

Mina wiped at the crumbs spilling on her skirt. "We're not sure." She glanced over to her mother who was visiting across the room. "We haven't heard from him in a long while."

It wasn't until after the meeting had ended and the ladies were dispersing that Tuva questioned Mina again. Mina carried the now sleeping toddler in her arms to the Thomsen's wagon while Tuva carried the baby.

"Tell me about your brother, Mina. What do you mean you're not sure where he is? How much older than you is he? What's his name?"

Mina laughed. "I don't believe I've ever heard you say that much at one time. Thorpe is twelve years older than me. I think my parents were quite surprised to have me come along that much later, but they assure me it was a nice surprise." She gave Tuva a mischievous grin as she handed the sleeping boy up to his mother now on the wagon seat. "Here you go, Mrs. Thomsen. My, he's getting big, isn't he?" She shook the numbness from the arm that had supported the sleeping child. "I'll talk to you later, Tuva. Will you be in town tomorrow? Maybe we could take a walk out to the Wheatly farm?"

Tuva spoke a few quiet words with her mother before answering. "I'm not sure if I can tomorrow, but soon. Bye, Mina."

Mina watched the wagon roll away with Tuva managing the reins and her mother balancing both the small children on her lap. The little boy had now awakened and was trying to climb up his mother's shoulder to wave goodbye. Mina waved.

The rest of the day passed by quickly with people to wait on and chores to do at the store. Mina was pleasant to the customers, but she knew not to gossip with them. That didn't mean she couldn't listen in on their conversations, however, and she picked up bits here and there about the telegram the Wheatlys received. The main consensus was that it had to be about their long-lost son. Telegrams usually meant bad news for someone, and Mina worried that the Wheatlys, who had borne so much hardship and worry already, were about to be faced with more. She determined that whether Tuva could join her or not, she was going to visit Helma and Thane on the morrow.

The following day brought rain and wind, causing Mina no end of frustration at being delayed in her mission. She hoped to hear word from a customer as to the nature of the telegram and spent much of the day helping in the store for that purpose.

Unfortunately, the weather also kept others indoors and few customers entered their door. The sun broke through by midafternoon, and Mina made up her mind to venture forth. She gained permission from her father to use the buggy, she packed a hamper of treats to bring to the couple, and she set out.

What she hadn't bargained on was the muddy condition of the roads after the rain. Mud clumps flew off the horse's hooves and the wheels sank into the ruts of the road. She struggled along, urging the horse to pull through the soft, sucking mud until eventually the wagon sunk too deep and the horse couldn't move it.

"Well, this is just dandy! What am I supposed to do now?" Mina looked around for help but saw no one. "There's nothing for it, but to push, I guess." She eyed the oozing ground around the buggy. Again she looked about. Making up her mind, she reached down and began undoing the buttons on her shoes. It took some time without a button hook, but she managed. Then she unrolled her long stockings and stuffed them inside the shoes and set them on the buggy seat. Next, she stood and took one more look around before lifting her skirts and tucking them into her waistband. Then she climbed down from the buggy.

Her bare feet sunk into the cold mud and she felt it ooze between her toes. She sank ankle deep in the goo as she made her way to the back of the buggy. She positioned herself to be ready to push before she called out to the horse. "Okay, Duncan! Go!" She pushed with all her might then realized that the horse hadn't made a move.

"Duncan! Don't be stubborn now! Move!" Again she pushed, and again the horse stood. He looked back over his shoulder as if to ask what she thought she was doing.

Mina wasn't about to give up. She had no whip to use on the animal. Gentle Duncan had never needed prodding, but something had to be done to get out of the slough they were in, so she looked around for a rock. She lurched as she felt a sharp stone under her foot, so she dug in the mud with her fingers until she grasped it.

"Sorry to do this, Duncan." She flung the rock, spattering her face with the mud that flew off her hand. It hit the horse on the flank and made him leap ahead, which pulled the buggy away as she was about to push it, causing her to fall forward into the mud as the buggy made it to higher ground. The horse kept running.

Mina scrambled to her feet. "Duncan, stop! Whoa! Whoa!"

Mud covered the entire front of Mina's shirtwaist and skirt as she tried to slop her way through the slough after the animal and buggy. She stumbled over hidden rocks and again lost her balance this time falling backward, landing with a splash.

If Tuva's mother saw me now, she wouldn't think much of me being an example to her daughter!

"Duncan!" Mina couldn't contain her frustration as she pulled herself upright and got to her feet again. "You stupid beast! Get back here!"

Suddenly a figure went running past her. She gasped as a voice beside her said, "Can I give you hand there, Miss?"

A tall, brown-haired man, his skin deeply tanned except for his cheeks and chin where a beard had obviously been, stood with his arm outstretched to take her hand. Mina reached for the hand and let the man pull her out of the mud onto solid ground. It was only then that she realized her skirt was still tucked into her waistband and her muddy legs from the knees down were exposed. She hastily released the skirt and it sloshed down, spattering the man's pant legs.

"Oh! I'm so sorry! Oh, look what I've done."

A noise farther up the road made her swing around abruptly, and she again sprayed the man with mud that flew from her clothing. But it was the sight of another man leading Duncan and the buggy back to them that had her attention.

"Duncan! Oh, thank you. Thank you, both. We got stuck in the mud, you see, and I couldn't get out and—"

"Yes, we saw."

Mina turned to the second man who was leading Duncan to her. He was of medium build, shorter than the first one. His face was also tanned very dark except under the red stubble of sprouting whiskers on his chin. He reminded her of someone.

"Do I know you?" She saw the man's eyes narrow as he studied her, looking for recognition.

"I don't think so, Miss—?"

He left the question hang until Mina understood he was asking her name. She was becoming aware of her appearance and the odd looks the men were giving her. She should be horrified to be caught in such a predicament, but for the moment it was all she could do to keep from laughing at the ridiculousness of the situation.

"Um...I'm Mina...I mean, I'm Wilhelmina...I mean..." She couldn't help it; she giggled.

"You okay, Miss?"

The honest concern was her undoing. She began laughing. The men smiled a little uncertainly at her and gave each other sideways glances that kept the laughter rolling out of her.

"You're not hurt, are you?"

They gave her a moment to catch her breath. The taller man seemed more amused than the other one, yet he kept silent, letting the other man ask the question. When Mina had quieted down, she tried making an apology.

"I'm so sorry...it's just that...well, look at me! And then, you two...you're trying to be so polite." She tried wiping away the tears her laughter had produced, but only succeeded in smearing the mud across her face. "I must look a sight!"

"On the contrary. I've never seen a lovelier, muddy person in my life." The taller man spoke the words so seriously that at first Mina was stunned. Then her lips turned upward as she caught the glint of humor in his eyes. She made a neat curtsy.

"Why, thank you, kind sir."

The tall man bowed in gentleman fashion. "May I present myself? I am Jacob Rodwell, and this is Keane Wheatly, Miss Mina Wilhelmina."

Mina spun around to Keane, missing the humorous way the man put her name. "Wheatly? Are you the son? I mean, are you—? Of course, you are!

You're Helma and Thane's son! You're alive! Oh, you don't know how they have worried about you. Are you going there now? Have you seen them yet? I was just on my way to visit them. You see, we heard they got a telegram. Oh, that must have been from you! But we were all worried that meant you were dead, and I was going to see if I could be of any help and—"

Keane took the hand that Mina had reached out to him. "Are they well?"

Mina stopped her rambling. "Yes. Oh, yes! They will be so happy to see you." Keane dropped her hand and Mina watched him rub his hands together to wipe off the mud she left on him. She turned to the man called Jacob Rodwell and noticed how much mud she had spattered on him. Her mud. She took a step away from them.

"I'm such a mess now that I will need to go home. Will you please take the basket from the buggy to your parents, Mr. Wheatly, and tell them I will visit another time after you have had a chance to greet them by yourself."

Keane seemed uncertain what to say. "You don't have to go. I mean, if you were headed to their house, we don't want to stop you."

But Mina was shaking her head. "No, please, I must return home and get cleaned up. Thank you again for bringing Duncan and the buggy back. Please give my regards to your parents, and...I am ever so glad that you have returned, Mr. Wheatly. Ever so glad!"

The brilliant smile she showered on him appeared to stun Keane. It was Jacob Rodwell who stepped forward to assist Mina into the buggy, ignoring the fact that he once again was splattered with the mud from her skirt as she swept it around her to climb up to the seat. She saw him eye her bare feet, and she tried to hide them under her skirt as she handed the basket for the Wheatlys back to him and thanked the two men again before flipping the reins and driving away.

After a hurried explanation to her parents about her appearance and her experience, Mina made it to her room to prepare for a well needed bath. She caught sight of herself in the mirror and stared at what she saw reflected. The mud-soaked skirt was probably ruined, her smeared face was comical, and the mud that dried on her feet made them as brown as an Indian's. The realization that the men had seen her like this dismayed her. *But why?* She asked herself. She had wanted to find out about Keane Wheatly because she cared about his parents. Why did it matter to her what he or that other man thought of her? What was the other man's name?

She held out her hands in front of her. He had taken her hand twice. She looked into the mirror again searching for an answer to why she was feeling so strange then she shook her head to dispel whatever fanciful thoughts were growing there.

I just want to know that the Wheatlys aren't worried anymore. That's all.

eight

Jake and Keane watched the buggy bounce away down the rutted road.

"That was interesting. Is Miss Wilhelmina someone from your childhood? She certainly seemed to recognize you."

Keane shook his head. "I don't think so. Funny thing about her name though. That's my mother's name. I wonder why she thought she knew me." He laughed as he pointed to Jake's clothing. "Which one of you was in the mud puddle?"

Jake tried brushing at the mud on his clothing but only managed to smear it worse. "She was like a cyclone, flinging mud in every direction. How did you escape?"

"Didn't." Keane pointed to the flecks of mud on his own clothing. He looked over his shoulder at the disappearing buggy. "She was a pretty thing though despite the mud."

Jake didn't reply out loud, but his thoughts were running along the same line as his friend's. To change the subject he pointed ahead. "How much farther?"

Keane started walking. "We're almost there now. See that turn in the road? My folks' acreage starts there. Looks like a good crop underway. I think they needed the rain. Hey, what's in that basket she left?"

Jake pulled aside the cloth covering the basket and found a treasure trove of cookies and breads. The two men lost no time in taking their fill as they walked along. The trip to Minnesota had gone better and easier than they expected. They did as Mr. Rogers suggested and left his horse in a neighboring friend's corral and then hiked the last mile or so to the railroad spur. The Great Northern Railroad took them all the way to their destination with only a couple of changeovers.

At first Jake had felt guilty about boarding the train secretly, but he understood the wisdom of Mr. Roger's suggestion. However, when he had the chance, he approached the train agent and paid him for their tickets, asking the man to let them stay in the baggage car. The man gave them no argument and asked them no questions. Whether he kept the money for himself or not, Jake didn't know and didn't care. He just felt better about it.

Jake could see the excitement growing in Keane as they approached the farm he had pointed out as *home*. They had sent a telegram ahead to prepare his parents, but no word was made of Jake coming along. He could only hope that his presence would not be a burden to the family. He would stay and help for a while until he decided what to do next.

"That's them!"

They were close enough now to see a man and woman come out the doorway and shield their eyes to see the travelers coming. Keane couldn't contain himself any longer and ran toward them. Jake kept walking, wanting to give them time alone before he entered the picture. He watched with joy the reunion between them, happy that he had a part in getting Keane back home.

"I have so much to tell you." Jake heard Keane's words as he stood back and waited, but when Keane saw him, he motioned him forward. "And this is the man who made it possible for us to escape and get here. This is my friend Jake Rodwell. Jake, these are my parents."

Jake extended a hand to Mr. Wheatly and was met with a firm handshake. He turned to Mrs. Wheatly and removed his hat. She held out her hand, a bit bewildered, it seemed, at all her son had been telling them, but soon had the two men inside and seated at the table with coffee cups in front of them along with fresh bread and jam.

Keane talked rapidly, telling them the story of the nearly two years he had been away in a matter of minutes. "So you see, that's why you never heard from me. Jake here was on board ship even longer than I was, and it was because of him we managed to finally escape. That was something!" And he continued the tale while the older couple sat transfixed, exhibiting shock, horror, joy, and tears throughout.

"I asked Jake to stay with us for now. He's willing to help out with the farm and all, and he really had nowhere else to go. See, his family is dead—"

Jake cleared his throat to interrupt. "I do not wish to intrude. I can certainly find accommodations in town."

The Wheatlys had barely spoken since their arrival, so caught up in Keane's story, but now Thane held up his hand to stop both men from saying more.

"You'll be most welcome to stay here, Jake. We are grateful to you for bringing our son home to us, and even though we don't know or understand all that's happened, we see that you've both been through a very bad time. No, you stay here as long as you want. You belong here."

Mrs. Wheatly was nodding her head and wiping tears from her eyes at the same time. She stood. "I will have supper ready soon. Have you had a lunch then?" She pointed to the basket.

"Oh, that's from some girl who was on her way out here to see you. She said her name was Wilhelmina. She was stuck in the mud and we helped her out. That's why Jake is covered in mud. She was quite a mess."

"Mina? She was coming here? That sweet girl! I hope she comes again soon because I want you to meet her. She and Tuva Thomsen have been coming to visit me. Such wonderful girls. Now, you go show Jake where to put his things in his room. Since we got your telegram we've been preparing for you to come home, and I'll just get busy cooking for you two. You look like you need food and plenty of it."

Keane led Jake upstairs to where two rooms were joined by a curtained doorway. "This one is mine." Keane stood with his hands on his hips and shook his head. "Ma kept it just like it was when I left." He pointed to the first room. "You mind having the one right off the stairway? If I come in after you, I might disturb you, you know." He grinned.

"It's a fine room, Keane." Jake stood in the center of the room, the only area he could stand upright for the ceiling slanted to the wall, where the bed was tucked in. "Thank you. I wonder what it will feel like to sleep in a real bed again. Looks like it's fit for a king."

"We'll have a lot of things to get used to again, I think." Keane slapped Jake on the back. "Here's where my clothes are. Help yourself to whatever fits you. I know we both are thin now, but Ma will see to it we get meat back on our bones, if I know anything." He pulled out some weathered clothing and tossed it on Jake's bed. "Trouble is, I'm shorter than you."

"Maybe I can get a few things in town one day."

"Yeah, that's a good idea. Well, I'll let you get changed. I'm going to have a look around the place. Come join me when you're ready."

Keane took off down the stairs two at a time in his haste to be back near his folks. Jake smiled to himself as he sat down on the bed. He stroked the colorful quilt covering and marveled at the softness. It was then that he noticed a Bible on the table beside the bed. His hand shook a little as he reached for it and ran his fingers over the leather cover. How long since he had held a Bible? Reverently he opened the book and paged through it. Before long he was deep in the passages he had relied on in his memory during the painful last three years. To see them again and to read them again brought tears to his eyes. How many times a day he quoted the same passages over and over in his mind to keep him focused on God and not on his surroundings! How they had brought him comfort during the most trying times of his life! And now, here they were, the verses in print before his eyes. He drank them in like a man dying of thirst reaches for life-giving water.

"Jake!"

He wiped at his eyes as Keane thundered up the stairway. Keane stopped suddenly on seeing Jake's tears and the Bible in his lap. His voice was quiet as he nodded to the book. "You find another sermon in there for me?"

Jake smiled at the question. During the three day trip by train, they had many discussions—sermons Keane called them—that bonded the two men even more than their shared imprisonment. It was during that time that Jake was able to show Keane the way of salvation.

"No," he answered Keane with a grin. "I found a sermon for me."

"You'll have to share it with me, brother," Keane was part teasing, part serious. "Come on, get changed. Ma's going to call us soon for supper, and you don't want to be late for one of Ma's suppers."

Jake set the Bible aside with reluctance but reminded himself that it was there any time. The feeling of freedom was still hard to grasp, and as he quickly changed into the clothing Keane had given him, he thanked the Lord again for their escape and for the comforts they had once again. He stood and looked down at the distance between the end of the pant legs and the floor and couldn't help chuckling. Life was good again.

Helma Wheatly outdid herself in preparing a homecoming meal for her son. Jake enjoyed every mouthful of the delicious chicken dinner, especially liking the creamed potatoes and peas that were set in a small bowl next to each plate. When Helma offered him second helpings, he gladly accepted.

"Told you Ma was a good cook." Keane beamed with pride, and Jake noticed that he often touched his dad's arm or gave his mom a quick hug as she passed by. Keane was reaffirming that he was home. Jake remembered Keane's fears that his parents, because of their ages, may not even still be alive.

Thane pushed back his chair. "I've got evening chores to do if you two would like to come along."

"Gladly, sir." Jake thanked Helma again for the meal, praising her cooking until the woman blushed with pleasure. Keane hugged his mother again and began telling Jake what the chores entailed as the men left the house.

The farm was not large, and it was evident that the older man had been managing, but there were many noticeable jobs waiting to be done. Thane even pointed some of them out.

"Sorry things have been getting away from me, but..."

"Now, don't you worry about that, Pa. I'm home now. Home for good. And with Jake's help, we'll get this place ship-shape again."

"Please don't say *ship*," Jake grimaced.

Keane slapped his friend on the back. "No, never again!" he agreed.

It was early the next morning that Keane tried tip-toeing past Jake's bed to the stairway, but Jake heard him.

"Time for chores?" Jake asked, starting to get up.

Keane put a hand on his friend's shoulder and whispered. "No. It's still way too early for the folks to be up. I...I just wanted some time to look around on my own. You don't mind, do you? I mean, you're welcome to join me..."

"Go ahead. Just get me when you need me, okay? I want to help out too."

"Oh, you will." Keane grinned in the gray light of morning at Jake. "Thanks. I'll see you later."

Keane was careful to avoid the squeaky spots on the stairway as he made his way quietly out of the house. He needed some time to be alone. For the last two years and even longer, he had someone working beside him, eating beside, even sleeping beside him. Come to think of it, it was only on this farm that he was truly able to be by himself. And he needed that. He needed space around him to think.

He made a quick survey of the barn and the corrals and the chicken coop, noting repairs that needed attention before he headed out into the fields and ran his hand along the spires of grain growing there. The field stretched before him in the morning dawn much like the ocean waves did from the deck of the ship. The memory made his fists clench at his sides, and suddenly he found himself running.

He ran until he came to the road and then he sprinted into an even faster pace. He didn't know how long he kept going before he slowed, his breath coming in gasps and his body dripping with sweat. He bent over and took deep breaths to cool off and to calm his rapid heartbeat. He didn't understand all that was going on inside him, but he figured that having the ability to physically move had to have something to do with experiencing his freedom again. On board the ship he couldn't run, he couldn't escape.

He stood straighter and looked around him. This part of the road was a hill and gave him an excellent view of the surrounding fields and farmland, the prairie grass and the trees in the distance. Land! He soaked it all in, enjoying the sights, the smells, and the sounds. Birds were beginning their morning wakeup calls, and he listened to their music with his eyes shut, trying to identify each song, each twitter, and each chirp.

He cocked his head to the side. *What?* There was another song coming from somewhere, but it wasn't from a bird. He looked side to side seeking the source of the lilting voice, and it was a voice—a human voice—he was hearing, he was sure. He followed the road until the sound became louder, though it was still soft, its melody almost blending in with the birds around it.

That tree.

Keane stopped and crouched down alongside the road. He remembered now. There was an old elm tree by the stream that ran by here. He listened again while he searched around the tree to see if someone was there. He could pick out some words now and recognized them from a hymn he had heard in church, but he still couldn't see anyone. He was held in place by the beauty of the voice blending in harmony with the songs of the birds. The dawning light of daybreak increased the volume of the song to a crescendo of praise to God as if it had been rehearsed to be in perfect time with the burst of the sun's rays across the fields.

Then the song stopped, though its final notes lingered in the air. Even the birds seemed to pause a moment before renewing their songs. It was then that Keane saw a girl swing herself down from a branch to the ground. She had been hidden from view by the fluttering leaves. The girl gave a quick look around her then walked swiftly away, following the side of the road until she was gone from view.

Keane rose from his hiding place and shielded his eyes from the sun to see if he could find her, but she was no longer there. It was almost as if he had dreamed it. He headed back to the farm feeling as though he had a glimpse of what heaven's music was like. He found Pa and Jake already in the barn starting on chores, and he made his apologies for being absent.

"Should have a good harvest this year," Pa was saying at breakfast later.

"Your soil certainly looks rich, and even though I don't know a lot about farming, I'd say the crops look mighty good to me." Jake broke open a biscuit and swabbed up the gravy from his plate. "Have you experienced bad crops?"

Keane gave a short laugh. "Pa could tell you stories. Go ahead, Pa, tell him about the grasshoppers."

Thane put his coffee cup down, but kept his work-gnarled hands around the cup as if to keep them warm. "First settlers here had it worse than I've had. I think it was about 1871 the first grasshopper plague came through. Those little beasts cleaned out the fields so there was nothing left. The next year they came again. The year after that the farmers needed to conserve their seed, so they only planted a small amount. No grasshoppers. So the next year they went ahead and planted, and the grasshoppers came again."

Keane spoke again. "If it wasn't for work on the railroads or the bonanza farms—those are the really large ones that require a lot of workers—Pa figures everyone would have had to leave the area just to survive. As it was, the work helped them get some wages to buy food until they could try again. Things have been pretty good since then."

"Don't forget the blizzard." Helma poured coffee as she made the comment.

"We had cold, bitter cold winters for several years and then in 1888, we had a nice, warm January day. Everyone was eager to get out and enjoy the warmth, the sun was shining and the snow was melting, but that afternoon the temperature dropped suddenly, the snow started, and the winds whipped up into a blizzard like we've never seen before."

Helma sat down. "Children were at school. Thankfully many teachers kept them in and rode out the storm, but others tried to get home and many were killed, lost in the snow, and frozen. It was terrible."

Jake was sober. "We heard the news in Seattle about the blizzard. That must have been awful."

"No worries, Jake, but you do have to be careful in the winter here. The snow blows across the prairie and the fields and you can't see two feet in front of you at times. That's why Pa has planted that row of trees for a windbreak. You'll see them all over by the farms here."

Thane rose to his feet. "We had a dry spell last year. Fire down in Hinckley killed about 400 people."

"No! How did that start?" Keane pushed back his chair.

"They think it was a spark off the trains. There's been a lot of logging down there and a lot of dead branches lying around that were quick to ignite."

"And the crops here? How did they do last year?"

Thane shook his head. "Not so good." He put his arm about his son's shoulders. "Good to have you back. We're going to have a good harvest this year."

Keane felt there was so much more his father was trying to say with the pressure of his arm about his shoulders. It must have been a hard couple of years for them while he was gone and no money coming in and the worry over their missing son. He shuddered to think what could have happened to his dear parents, but he had Jake—Jake and his God—to thank for getting him home again.

Not just Jake's God anymore. *His* God too.

The men kept busy all afternoon. Keane sent his father into the house to rest while he and Jake worked on fence repairs and other projects needing their attention. For the most part the men worked in silence, a habit ingrained in them from being on the ship, but later when they sat under the shade of a tree and enjoyed cold glasses of water brought to them by Helma, Keane told Jake what he had heard that morning.

"I don't know how to explain it, but it almost seemed like the birds were singing with her. And then when the sun burst into view...it was...it was...something!"

Keane's face grew hot as Jake stared at him. "Now, don't go making fun of me."

Jake shook his head. "I only wish I had seen and heard it too."

Still unsure if his friend was mocking him, Keane added, "I felt like I was in church."

"Well, you don't have to be in church to worship God, although assembling together with other believers is a privilege. The Bible says our bodies are the temple of the Holy Spirit, so wherever we are and whatever we do, we can worship him. It seems your *bird girl* expressed that quite well."

"I wonder who she is. Maybe she's new to the area. I've missed out on more than two years here, so a lot has probably changed, but I think I would have remembered hearing a voice like that." Keane stood and Jake followed suit, brushing any dirt from his trousers. Keane couldn't help laughing at the short-legged pants. "Next time Ma heads to town for supplies, we better go along and find you something to wear."

Jake grinned. "Good idea. And maybe you can spot your *bird girl* too."

Now Keane knew his friend was teasing. "Okay, enough of that. Or were you hoping to get a glimpse of your *mud girl*?"

A strange expression crossed the other man's face, and Keane wondered if he had gone too far. "Sorry, Jake. I didn't mean...I mean with your wife gone and all..."

"No, it's okay." Jake put his hand on Keane's shoulder. "She was a mess, wasn't she? By the way, is there a bank in Ulen? I didn't get much of chance to see anything the way you hurried us through there."

Keane shrugged. "Had to get home. You know how it was."

"I know."

They started back to the fence. "I don't know if there's a bank now or not, to tell the truth. I'll have to ask Ma."

Less than a week later, Keane declared that he had a list of supplies that they needed in order to complete some of the repairs on the farm, and he was ready to go to town to get them. He nearly missed the look that passed between his parents.

"Something wrong? Do you need me here, Pa?"

Thane reached for his coffee cup and entwined his fingers around it. Keane wondered if the heat from the coffee eased some of his dad's arthritis pain. He waited, knowing there was something his father wanted to say. An uneasy feeling came over him.

"What's wrong?"

"Like I said before, crops weren't too good last year. We borrowed from the merchants for supplies for this year, but we can't pay what we owe until after harvest. We can't afford to buy any more on credit right now. Those repairs and things will have to wait. Sorry, son."

"But—" Keane dropped into a chair with a thud, stunned by what he heard. He covered his face with his hand. "It's my fault. It's all my fault."

"No, Keane—"

But Keane shook his head and faced his father. "I could have sent you more money. I…I started spending some on myself. That's how I ended up—I was so stupid! I got what I deserved! But you didn't deserve to have to suffer because of it. I'm so sorry, Pa."

Keane hadn't heard Jake come into the room, but he felt his friend's presence behind him. "It's no one's fault, Keane. Don't dwell on it. Like I told you, we have to forget and move on. You have a new life in Christ, a life with a purpose." He turned to Thane. "I have some money, enough for the supplies we need—"

He was cut off by Thane rising to his feet. "I will not take money from you. If anything, we owe you for saving our son's life!"

"But you have it wrong, sir. Keane saved my life that night in the storm as well. We couldn't have gotten away without each other. This money I have...it's not even really my money."

Keane stood. Something in Jake's voice bespoke an inward pain. He saw his friend's hesitation. "You don't have to tell us, Jake."

"No, I want to. I've wanted to tell someone for a long time because...because I can't tell *them* anymore."

Helma came into the room, wiping her hands on her apron, her face full of concern at the tension she saw in the young man's face.

"Please, sit down, Mrs. Wheatly—I mean, Helma. You too, Thane. Keane. My story isn't very pleasant to tell, and I am ashamed you have to hear it, but I've been rescued by God's grace time and time again, so this is just another one of those times." Jake smiled slightly before continuing. "My parents were good, godly people, wealthy people. I grew up lacking nothing, but as with so many young, foolish people, I wasn't satisfied. I guess because I had everything, I went looking for things I didn't have. And I found them. Like the prodigal son, I wasted my substance by riotous living. But unlike the prodigal, I didn't return to my parents."

Jake covered his eyes with his hand briefly before resuming his story. "Funny thing was, I didn't want to disrespect my parents, so I changed my name. Still, they found me. They sent me money, pleading with me to come home. I refused. It was Eva, my wife, who showed me the love Jesus Christ had for me, a love I in no way deserved. He died for my sins.

That's such a simple statement, but it changed my life completely. I placed my faith in that fact. I believed he not only died for my sins, freeing me from their guilt forever, but that he rose from the dead as well." Jake chuckled. "I never had to be told that it wasn't my good deeds that would get me into heaven, because I had no good deeds that would please God. I knew my sinfulness. Oh, I knew!

"Then I got word that my parents had died. That was a blow to me because I didn't have the chance to go to them and accept the love they kept trying to show me. I didn't get the chance to let them meet my wife before she died. The money is my inheritance from them. It's more than I need or deserve, as I said. Please allow me to share it with you."

Thane started to shake his head, but Jake forestalled him from speaking.

"Being here is therapeutic. You are giving me the time I need to stand once again on my own. My body has been physically abused, but my mind has been too." He clapped Keane's shoulder. "Scars need time to heal, and some, like the ones left on our backs from Thor's whip, will never go away, but they will be a reminder to keep trusting our savior." Then he cleared his throat and grinned. "Besides, you told me to feel like family and family helps each other. Now, not another word about money."

The Wheatlys looked at each other a moment then Thane stood once again. "I'll help you hitch up the wagon, boys. Helma, you better get your bonnet if you're going to town."

nine

Mina tried to hide her frustration at being kept so busy at the store. The beautiful weather that followed the rainstorm was bringing in every customer from round about the town. She was kept busy exchanging housewives' goods for merchandise and staples. Depending on what the farm produced, she found herself counting out eggs or weighing slabs of butter or rounds of cheese or hanging hams in the storeroom to be exchanged for flour or sugar or spices. She filled the jars the women brought in with vinegar or maybe kerosene. She ground coffee beans and measured out bolts of fabric. She weighed out peanut butter and rice and oatmeal and candy. All the while she was wondering what was going on at the Wheatly farm.

Keane looked just like the picture Helma showed me. Only older.

He was thin, but he looked strong. The same with the tall man. *What's his name? Jake something?*

"No, Miss Prescott, I said half a pound, not a whole pound, please."

"Sorry, Ma'am." Mina scolded herself for not paying attention. Mother wasn't feeling well, and that meant Father needed help in the store, but Mina was having trouble concentrating when her mind was on Helma and how happy she must be to have her son home again. She couldn't help but wonder what had kept him away so long. She listened to the conversations going on in the store to see what she could find out but could hear nothing about the Wheatlys other than speculations. Even Tuva didn't seem to know when she stopped by that morning.

"But hasn't anyone gone over there?" Mina asked her friend. "You don't live very far away, why don't you go? Bring them a cake or something to welcome their son home."

Tuva's expression was incredulous. "*I'm* not going over there. Really, Mina, everyone is busy right now getting ready for harvest. The Wheatlys will show up in town eventually. Why do you care so much anyway?"

"I'm curious; that's all. Aren't you?"

A voice called from across the room. "Mina!"

"I've got to help Father. Let me know as soon as you hear anything, Tuva." Mina hurried to help her father behind the counter, missing the puzzled expression on Tuva's face.

It was later that day when she was backing out of the storeroom while trying to roll a pickle barrel on its edge across the floor to its place beside the counter that she heard a voice behind her.

"I see you got the mud off."

Mina looked back over her shoulder and lost her grip on the barrel. The barrel slid a few inches before landing squarely on her toe.

"Ow!" She pushed the barrel forward, nearly upsetting it and let it drop again. Unfortunately, she had already loosened the top of the keg, and pickle juice was sent sloshing down both sides of the barrel and over her dress. The aroma of vinegar and dill filled the air.

Mina stood still. She raised her chin enough to see Keane Wheatly's astonished face, and behind him the tall man she thought was named Jake swiping his hand across his face to hide a grin. Both seemed to be waiting for a response from her.

"Pickles anyone?" She raised her eyebrows in question.

Mina's father finished with a customer and stepped over to see what had happened. "Mina, your dress! You better go change. I'll clean this up. Hello, gentlemen, may I be of service?"

The two men seemed to have a hard time taking their attention from Mina's predicament, but Keane pulled a list from his pocket and handed it to the man.

"I see." Mina's father scanned the list while Mina made her way to the stairway leading to the living quarters above the store. She felt the tall man was still watching her, and when she glanced back, she caught his eye. He nodded and smiled.

Mina took the stairs quickly as she heard her father say, "Yes, I have some of these things, but you may have to check with the Evanson Brothers or the Olson's for the hardware you need. If you'll step over here..."

Her father's voice faded as Mina reached the top step and entered their sitting room. She raced to her bedroom and pulled off the soiled garment. She dressed again as swiftly as she could so she could get back downstairs and hear what was going on. A quick look in the mirror and she hurried to the stairway. She made herself slow down the last few steps. There was no need to break a leg too.

Father was still assisting the two men, so Mina grabbed a towel and began wiping up the pickle juice while she watched and listened to them. Another customer came in and took Mina's attention away. She looked up when the bell on the door sounded in time to see Keane's back as he left the store. She hid her frustration at missing out on the conversation as she counted out the change to her customer. When the tall man spoke from the end of the counter, she turned in surprise, thinking he had walked out ahead of Keane.

"What?"

"I said hello."

"Oh." Mina approached him. "Hello. I'm sorry, I forgot your name."

"Jake. Jake Rodwell. And you're Mina Wilhelmina? Odd name."

"I'm what? No. I'm Mina. I mean I'm Wilhelmina, but everyone calls me Mina."

"How do you do, Mina? Or is that too familiar? Should I say Miss Austinson or is it Miss Asleson? Both names appear on the sign outside."

Mina was a little flustered at his attention and was about to correct him about her name, when she saw he was about to step in a puddle of pickle juice she hadn't wiped up. "Look out there! Oh!"

She stopped herself from saying any more, because it was then that she noticed how short his pant legs were. She tried not to look, but couldn't help it.

Jake seemed not to mind at all. He put his hands in his pockets and pulled up even more on the pant legs. "Something wrong, Miss Mina? You don't like my trousers?"

Just then Mina's father came by with a stack of men's trousers in his hands. "Here you go, Mr. Rodwell. This is what we have in your size."

Mina stepped away as the two men went through the stack, and Jake held them up to check for length. She was full of questions as to why he didn't have proper clothing that fit him and needed to buy some. And what was he doing with Keane Wheatly? And where had Keane been all this time?

She pretended to straighten shelves as she listened to Jake talk with her father, but nothing was mentioned other than the purchases until Jake said, "Mrs. Wheatly will be in shortly to get supplies. I would like to put some money on their account to cover the cost, and could you tell me what is owed on their account so that I can cover that as well, please?"

Mina's eyes widened in surprise. The store was operated mostly on credit with the bills not being paid until after harvest. To have someone pay with cash now was unusual. She watched as her father turned the account book for Jake to inspect the figures then saw Jake hand over several bills to her father.

"That should take care of it and add some to the account. I would appreciate you keeping this between us, sir."

"Of course, young man. Glad to be of service. If there is anything else you need, please let me know."

"Thank you. Good day, sir." Jake turned and caught Mina's eye. "Good day to you, Miss Mina."

Mina nodded with a slight smile. She looked questioningly at her father after Jake had gone, but he only shrugged and put the account book away.

It wasn't long until Helma came in and while her father was busy filling the order on her list, Mina wasted no time asking the woman about her son's return, noting that the worry had gone from her friend's face.

"God does indeed answer prayer, Mina. Keane is home! He's had a bad time of it, I'm afraid, but he'll recover. He found himself a good friend in Jake Rodwell, and I thank the Lord for that. The best news of all, Mina, is that Keane came to know the Lord while he was away!"

Mina's hug was spontaneous and she listened with rapt attention as Helma told about how Jake had shown Keane the way of salvation through Jesus Christ. "We always just assumed Keane understood how to get saved, you know. After all, he'd been to church with us since he was a baby, but it's a good lesson for all of us to learn that each one of us has to make a decision to accept Christ by faith. We can't just think we're saved because we go to church."

Helma talked a little more until her order was filled. "I must go meet up with the boys and let them know they can load the order now. It was so good to see you, Mina. You stop in and see me again, will you?" She turned to Mina's father. "Will you be good enough to put this on our account, Mr. Prescott? We'll be paying up after harvest, and thank you again for your patience with us."

Mina watched her father confirm to the woman that all would be handled according to her wishes. Even though Mina was excited with Helma's news, she was frustrated because she didn't get any of her questions answered about where Keane had been all this time. And now she had more questions about Jake Rodwell and how he had money to pay the Wheatlys' bill.

"Curiosity killed the cat, you know."

Mina sighed as she smiled at her father. "I know. I should. You remind me nearly every day!"

"Why do you always want to know about everybody and everything, little Mina?"

"I don't know, but isn't it curious—?"

She stopped and looked at her father and they both burst out laughing. "Looks like we have a break for a bit. Why don't you go up and see how your mother is feeling?"

Mina had hoped to be around when Jake and Keane loaded Helma's order, but she obeyed her father, thinking he was probably aware that was what she was hoping. She found her mother resting in her bedroom.

"How are you feeling, Mother? Can I get you anything?"

She sat down on the edge of the bed and noticed the furrow between her mother's eyes. "Does your head ache?"

"It does a bit, but I'm all right, dear. How are things going downstairs?"

Mina told her mother about the pickle barrel.

"So that's why I heard you up here. Oh, Mina! You're always in a pickle!"

Her mother's eyes widened when she realized what she said, and both women laughed.

"It's either a pickle puddle or a mud puddle!"

Mrs. Prescott smiled at her daughter. "Mina, you are so good for me. I only wish…" She looked down at an envelope in her hand.

It was the first that Mina had noticed it. "What is it, Mother? Did you get a letter from someone? Bad news?"

"No, nothing to worry about. You'd better go see if your father needs you now. Thank you for checking on me."

Mina backed slowly out of the room, but her mother's eyes remained closed. There was something in that letter that was bothering her. Did Father know? What could it be?

Harvest time was such a busy time throughout Ulen that Mina had no chance to visit at the Wheatlys. She did go once in hopes of learning more about Keane and Jake, but Helma had canning jars lined up in the kitchen and was preparing meals to take to the men in the fields and had no time for a leisure talk. Mina offered her assistance but only found herself in the way as the woman hurried about her tasks.

Tuva kept Mina company when she was free, which was seldom. She had agreed to help get a school started in Walworth Township but didn't plan on being the teacher.

"Mother needs help with the smaller children at home," she explained to Mina. "I may teach another year."

Once again Mina felt a bit left out, even useless compared to the hard-working men and women around her. She expressed her feelings to her mother.

"I know there's plenty to do at the store and always something to clean, but I'd like to do more social things with people. It just seems that everyone is too busy for that here."

"Harvest is almost over so things will settle down," her mother assured her. "In fact, I heard some of the ladies talking about a basket social."

"What's that?"

"Each lady in the community, whether married or not, prepares a basket lunch and then the men make bids for it. The money raised is used for town projects like supplies for the schools and such."

"What happens when the man gets the basket?" Mina had never heard of such a thing.

"Then he and the lady who prepared it sit down together and have lunch. I hear that wives show their husbands the baskets they prepare so that they bid on the right ones."

"You mean they pay to eat their own food?"

"It's a fund raiser, dear. Doesn't it sound like fun?"

Mina frowned slightly. "Seems like a lot of foolishness just to raise money, especially if people are buying their own food and then paying for it twice."

"Ah, but not everyone knows whose basket is whose. The bachelors and the young ladies pair off to eat lunch together and get acquainted." Her mother watched Mina for a reaction.

"Oh." Then Mina's eyes widened. "Oh! But what if someone bids on your basket and you don't want to eat with them? What if—? When is this going to be?"

"Saturday, behind the Bethlehem Church."

Mina grew excited. "Mother, may I take the buggy to go to the Thomsen's? Tuva will have all the details and—"

"I just saw Tuva walk past the City Hotel. Go on." Mrs. Prescott laughed.

Mina raced out the door, nearly knocking down a couple walking by. She spotted the tall form of her friend headed north toward the post office and hurried to catch up to her. A few moments later they were walking side by side and Mina was peppering Tuva with questions about the basket social.

"I don't know why you're so excited about it, Mina. It's just something we do now and then for a fund raiser."

"Well, tell me about it. What kind of basket do you make? What do you put in it? Who bids on it? Is it awkward?"

Tuva was shaking her head before Mina could finish. "I've never put a basket in the auction. I just eat with my folks because my mom always fixes enough for all of us."

Mina stopped walking and stared at Tuva in amazement. "But why don't you make a basket? Aren't we supposed to? I mean, should I or shouldn't I? I don't understand."

Tuva gave a half shrug of her shoulders. "You can if you want to, Mina. I just don't because I don't want to be stuck eating with some old bachelor." A train stopping at the depot made conversation nearly impossible so the two girls waited and watched with others as some men got off and began walking to the City Hotel, some stopping to lift their hats at the ladies and address people on the streets. Most all carried a case of some kind or other. Tuva pointed.

"And sometimes those salesmen off the train hang around at our social events. I certainly don't want to end up sharing a lunch with one of them."

"Oh." Mina nodded slightly in understanding. "But...well...what's the point of doing it at all if no one puts a basket up for auction?"

Tuva began moving again, making Mina skip a step to stay with her. "Lots of the women and the young girls put baskets in, Mina. I'm just one of the ones who doesn't."

Mina stopped again and put her hand on Tuva's arm to stop her as well. "It's just because you're so shy, and...I think maybe you've been waiting for someone special to be here to bid on your basket."

Tuva gave an unladylike snort. "What? I don't know what you're talking about. You put one in for yourself if you want to, but leave me out of it."

"No, wait! I have an idea." Mina was all smiles. "Let's both put baskets in." She waved away Tuva's protests. "And if we don't like who bids on them, I'll have one of the young schoolboys around here outbid them and we can eat together. What do you say?"

"The kids don't have enough money for that."

"No, silly, I know that. I'll give them some money. It's for a good cause, right?"

Tuva frowned at her. "Why are you so set on this? Who is it that you want to buy your basket?"

Mina shook her head. "I really don't know. I just want to join in the fun."

After more pleading and cajoling Tuva finally gave in and agreed to go along with Mina's plan. "But I'm telling you right now to have one of the boys bid on it. I'm not taking any chances."

Mina began planning what to put in her basket right away. From some of the customers she learned that special ribbons decorating the baskets would give the gentleman they wished to purchase it, a clue as to whose basket it was. She overheard some of the young ladies talking.

"I hinted to Clarence that the blue ribbon on the basket would match the blue ribbon on my hat. He better have more money this year. Last year he quit bidding at fifteen cents and ended up eating with Widow Hetley."

"Who got your basket?" Another girl asked.

"My brother." She rolled her eyes. "He knew I baked a special pie and he wanted it."

They moved on as Mina smiled at the comments. Maybe she would decorate hers to match her hat as well. Though she hadn't actually admitted it, even to herself, she hoped that Jake or Keane would be her lunch partner. She had so many questions to ask.

ten

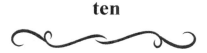

Thorpe stared out the train window without seeing the passing scenery. His thoughts were filled with what he had learned about Wheatly and Rodwell.

He sent men searching for any information that might tell him the two men had survived the storm in the little rowboat, and he got some answers that convinced him they were alive. The men reported back to him at the hospital what they had learned.

First, he had them go from house to house along the coastline, asking questions to see if anyone had helped the two men. He soon learned that people were unwilling to give answers, whether they knew anything about the men or not. Even when Thorpe's men tried to convince them that they were searching for their fellow seamen and were worried for their lives, the residents were uncooperative. Too many of them were aware of the evil practice of shanghaiing to believe what the men said.

Then Thorpe tried a different angle. He inquired of the crimps he knew worked the area about the time Wheatly was brought on board ship. Being a crimp once himself, he knew how they did their dirty business. There was a lack of men signing on to work the ships, especially as it was learned that the boarding masters would by trickery keep the man's first few months' pay for himself, and legislation made it illegal for a man to leave the ship or he would be imprisoned. When men stopped signing on voluntarily, the boarding master—or crimp—would coerce a man or more likely, render him unconscious, forge his signature on the ship's articles, and collect his *blood money* for producing the man to the ship's captain. Crimps were paid by the body, so they used any trick they had to get sailors on ships.

Thorpe had his men search the area for anyone with the name Wheatly, but they turned up nothing. Then he learned that about the time that Wheatly came on board, the railroad crew was finishing up the Great Northern line in Seattle, and some of the newly shanghaied men were from the railroad crew. One of Thorpe's men located the former railroad boss, bought him a few drinks, and got him talking about the men on his work team. It took a while to get Wheatly to come to the man's memory, but eventually he remembered Wheatly having a friend named Smitty, whom he recalled as always being a complainer.

"Smitty didn't like any of the jobs. Nothing was good to him, so it's funny that he's still here working for the railroad. You just can't make sense of some people."

Smitty was located and questioned and after being paid a handsome sum, "remembered" that Keane Wheatly was from a farm near a small town in western Minnesota.

Excited by this progress, Thorpe sent his men looking into Rodwell and learned that the name was familiar in the area. Word came back to him that three or four years ago a woman named Eva Rodwell had died. The doctor who had this information was able to tell Thorpe's man where the homestead was, and Thorpe decided to make a visit there himself.

His arm was still bandaged and painful but not noticeable under the larger coat he wore. The rest of his appearance gave no indication of his injury, but his tanned features gave evidence of his time on the open water. He stepped down from the landau he had rented, being careful not to use his left arm.

Thorpe spotted the little boy at the window of the small house and smiled. A woman's face appeared briefly, pulling the boy away, and then the door opened.

"Yes, sir?"

Thorpe removed his hat. He was a handsome man and displayed gentlemanly manners that would be unrecognizable to the seamen who had the misfortune to serve under him. "Good day, Madam. Hello, young sir. Do I have the pleasure of meeting the wife of my cousin Jacob Rodwell?"

The woman seemed confused, unsure how to answer. "Uh, no sir, I'm Mathea. Mathea Dorkin."

"How do you do, Mrs. Dorkin. Would Mr. and Mrs. Rodwell be at home?"

Mathea bit at her lower lip. "Uh, well sir, they don't live here anymore. My husband and I do."

Thorpe expressed his surprise. "But I was informed that this was the residence of Jacob Rodwell and his wife Eva Rodwell."

Mathea reached for her son and brought him closer to her. "No. Not anymore."

Thorpe frowned. "Do you know where I might find them? You see, I've traveled quite a distance to talk to my cousin Jacob. I'm afraid I have some troubling news to give him and the family wished it to be delivered in person rather than through a telegram. There's been a death in the family, you see, and I have some inheritance to pass on to Jacob."

Thorpe watched indecision cross over Mathea's face. "If you have any idea of how I could find him, it would sure help."

"I don't know where he went, but..." Mathea looked hard at Thorpe. "Since you're his cousin and all, I guess it wouldn't hurt to tell you that he took his papers from here and was going to the bank. Maybe they know more. That's all I can tell you."

He was here! "Papers?"

Mathea nodded. "We found some bank papers that belonged to him, and we kept them safe in case he came looking for them, and he did. He and an older woman came."

Thorpe was able to get the name of the bank from the young mother, thanked her, and headed back to town.

An older woman? Now who could that be?

The man at the bank was of no help, so much so that Thorpe suspected that he was purposely withholding information. It was easy to bribe a young employee to look into the matter and report back that Jacob Rodwell had indeed been there and had withdrawn a considerable sum of money. That worried Thorpe because it meant the man had means to travel anywhere and be lost to him, but he still had another clue.

It was one of the crimps who reported seeing a man and an older woman leave the bank on the day Thorpe mentioned.

"Seemed kind of nervous, he did. I didn't know the woman, but I've seen that horse and wagon down by the docks many a time. There's a man named Rogers who was always asking about his son and threatening to search every ship that came into port. 'Course we kept him out of the way."

"Rogers? Do you know where he lives?"

"No, but I can find out."

Again, Thorpe made the trip himself. The Rogers' cabin was located in an area that the escaped men could have found had they made shore there. He was getting close, but he had to be careful. His men told him that Rogers' son had also been shanghaied, and even though Thorpe had no memory of him, it meant the couple could be antagonistic and evasive concerning questions about the two men. He'd have to approach them in a different way.

The cabin was modest, and the couple who opened the door to him were of pioneer stock, hardy and hard-working. He lifted his hat.

"Pardon my intrusion. Are you Mr. and Mrs. Rogers?"

The man nodded and the woman eyed him with suspicion, a sign that she had something to hide. "What is it?"

Thorpe kept his tone businesslike. "I understand that your son is a sailor."

The couple made no reply.

"We have reason to believe that some of the men who have signed on to ships have been forced to do so against their will. May I ask if you have had word from your son?"

The man's arm reached behind the door and when he stepped forward, he was holding a shotgun in his arm. "What do you want?"

"Now, hold on there, Mr. Rogers. I'm here to help. If you believe your son has been coerced, then we can take legal action against the ship's owner and get his release. I have been sent to inquire of people in the area who wish to make such claims."

"We're making a claim, alright. We're suing the owner for the death of our Tommy."

Tommy. Tom Rogers.

Thorpe remembered now. The kid who went overboard, trying to escape. He had him and another man dragged under the ship until they drowned. *He was their son.*

A twitch of his eye was the only indication that Thorpe was affected by the name. He stayed true to his masquerade. "I am sorry for your loss, truly I am. I beg your forgiveness for intruding on the memory of your son, but you see, this is exactly why I have been sent. We want to help families like yours and hopefully save some of these unfortunate men. If you know of anyone else who needs our help, please let me know. There will be monetary compensation, and I will see to it personally that you are given the share that your son would have had."

He turned to go then stopped. "May I ask, how did you learn of your son's death? It has been very difficult for me to get any answers from the owners or dock workers."

The shotgun was moved to the man's side as he looked to his wife and received a nod from her. "Heard about it when that last ship came in, the one that was burned."

"Ah, yes. We were able to help rescue several men from that one and get them help. Such a tragic thing. We learned that some of the men tried escaping the fire in a rowboat, but apparently they were all drowned. We have had no word that any survived."

Silence.

Thorpe waited a few moments then touched the brim of his hat. "Again, my condolences. You will be hearing from me when we get this matter settled. Good day."

He rode away from the cabin, noting that they watched him leave. When out of sight, he stopped the horse and made his way on foot back to the cabin. He kept hidden and quiet as he waited and listened and soon he was rewarded when the cabin door opened and the couple came out.

"I still don't believe he was here on behalf of Tommy. Something wasn't right about it. I think he was fishing for information about Keane and Jake." The woman stood in the doorway and spoke to her husband as he walked to the woodpile and picked up the axe.

"We'll not hear from him again." He swung the axe, splitting a log. "I'm just glad those two are safe on Keane's farm. I've half a mind to pick up stakes and move to Minnesota myself. I have no longing to see the ocean anymore, knowing Tommy's fate."

It was enough. Thorpe made his way back to the rented landau and planned his next steps as he drove back to town. He had made quite a fortune for himself, first as a crimp, and then as a first mate on the ship. He enjoyed the control he had over the men, the power. But laws were changing and legislation being passed to prosecute officers guilty of mistreating seamen. He should move on while he can. There was always work for men like him, and he had several followers who would work with him.

The train sped on. It hadn't been too hard to find the conductor who was willing, for a price, to tell him exactly where the men had gotten off the train.

They got off in Fargo, North Dakota, but the Rogers said the farm was in Minnesota.

He'd have to send some men around to ask questions.

Once he was finished with his business he'd go on down to Ohio and see his folks. *How many years has it been?* He did some quick calculations. He'd left home when he was sixteen and hadn't looked back. He was now thirty-one. *Has it really been fifteen years?* He thought of his little sister with the big name. Wilhelmina was what? Three or four then? Other than a few occasional letters to ask his folks to send him some money, he had no idea what his family was doing.

But first, he would deal with Wheatly and the preacher. No one gets the best of Thorpe Prescott.

eleven

"What are you doing there, Ma?"

Keane came up behind his mother and peered over her shoulder. He reached for one of the cookies she was wrapping in paper, but she slapped his hand away.

"These are for the basket social tomorrow. I set some on the table for you and Jake."

"Be sure to put in enough for all of us. I don't plan on taking a chance of eating with some young kid or worse, some husband-seeking female."

"It wouldn't hurt for you to do a little socializing and get to know some of the young ladies in the area. I'm not getting any younger, and I'd like to bounce a grandchild or two on my knee someday." Helma's lifted eyebrows demanded a response from her son.

"I know, Ma, but you're going to have to give me time. I mean...I'm still having nightmares from what I've gone through, and truthfully, I don't know if I'll ever stop having them. It's not easy to get here—back home, I mean—and continue on with my life as if nothing has happened. I don't know how to act anymore. I keep looking over my shoulder expecting someone to drag me back there."

Helma reached for Keane and held him to her. "They wouldn't, would they? They can't. You're safe now, and you take all the time you need. There's no hurry about finding a girl. Pa and I are just glad you're back and that you're safe, and all we want is for you to be happy again."

"I am, Ma. I'm happier than I've ever been. Just give me some time, okay?"

She nodded and returned to packing the basket. "Don't worry, I've put plenty of food into this basket, enough to feed us and more. It will be good to take a day off and relax. You men have been working too hard."

Jake entered the side door to the kitchen in time to hear Helma's comment. "I think you're the one who has been working too hard, Helma. I've seen the rows of canning jars in the root cellar. You're up before we are and you're the last one to bed." He peeked into the basket on the counter. "What's this about a basket social?"

Keane took over the explanation, ending by saying, "You can bid if you want to, but I'm aiming to sit with my Ma. I know how good her cooking is."

Helma beamed at the praise. "You are welcome to join us, Jake. I'll have plenty."

Jake thanked her, but later when he was working beside Keane in the barn, he asked. "What did you mean I could bid if I want to? Have you bid before?"

Keane laughed. "I did once before I left. I thought it was going to be—well, never mind who I thought it was going to be. The basket turned out to be a school girl's. A freckled-face, pigtailed school girl! She tagged around behind me after that until her mother got after her. It was embarrassing. Quit laughing."

Jake's chuckles made Keane smile.

"Just think, Keane, she's a little older now. Maybe she's even your singing *bird girl*."

"Aw, cut it out. Besides, I told Ma I wasn't ready for any of that stuff yet." He grew serious. "We've been through an awful time, you and me, and I for one do not feel I can handle anything more than seeing the sunrise each day and knowing I'm alive and free to enjoy it."

"But there's something else I think of." Jake stopped his work to look at Keane. "Life can be over so quickly. It's been more than three years now that my wife went to Glory. Every day that we were on that ship I thought would be my last. But it wasn't. And now I want to put that behind me and live each day to please God. I don't know what tomorrow will bring, but I'm not going to live in fear or in dwelling on the past. Like you said, I'm enjoying each new sunrise."

The men went back to work in silence until Keane asked, "So, are you going to bid on *mud girl's* basket?"

Jake found the town's basket social to be very interesting. He strolled around the grassy lawn, watching and listening to the talk going on and felt a long awaited peace fill him. He was a curiosity, but people were too polite to question him. Keane, on the other hand, was welcomed with back slaps and handshakes. Some knew by now what had happened to the two men. Others still wondered, Jake could tell by their expressions.

The day, late into August, promised to be hot. Women were fanning themselves, and everyone was seeking the shade of the surrounding elm trees. Jake found a spot a little away from the others where he was shaded and felt a light breeze now and then. He could still hear and see what was going on. The ice wagon was on hand to provide a chill to the lemonade and water, and Jake watched the young boys sneak chunks of ice. He envied the thieves who ran away, licking the frozen treat.

Mr. Wiger, the township clerk, gave some announcements and introduced the new schoolteachers for some of the surrounding areas. He made a big speech about how all the funds raised would be to help purchase needed school supplies. Then there was some music, some young girls recited poetry, and a woman of considerable girth sang a patriotic song. All this was to lead up to the main event, the auctioning of the baskets.

Jake learned more about what to expect as he had roamed around the picnic area. Helma herself had given some clues when she carefully had Thane examine her basket so that he would be sure to bid on the right one. It was supposed to be a secret who made the baskets, but Jake caught on quickly to certain ladies pointing out a ribbon in their hair to a male admirer who quickly scanned the baskets looking for an identical ribbon. When the man knew which one it was, he would signal with a wink or a nod to the young lady, so that she would know he was ready.

It was comical yet sweet to Jake to watch. Most secretive of all were the baskets the new school teachers brought. The bachelors were getting their first glimpse of the newest single women in town and were craning their necks to hunt for clues on the baskets to see if any matched the young ladies. Of particular interest was Mina. She appeared bearing no basket in hand, but a flower in her hair was noticed immediately. There were many perplexed faces as several baskets sported the same flower.

Jake watched Mina visit with a tall girl. The girl's Scandinavian heritage stood out in her blonde, braided hair. She had an unmistakable beauty, yet she seemed completely unaware of it. Mina was in contrast to her only in the dark color of her hair and her shorter stature. Mina was entirely lovely in her own way.

Jake was startled by his thoughts. To his astonishment he felt no guilt in being attracted to the young ladies. He knew that meant he was healing from the wounds of losing Eva and the life and death horror he had faced for so long. He took a deep breath. That didn't mean he was going to start anything. He was just here to watch and learn and adjust to normal life again.

Mina was now talking earnestly with a young boy, and Jake saw her point toward the tables that held the baskets. Then Mina handed the boy some money.

What is she up to?

It was time to begin. Mr. Wiger emphasized the importance of giving generously to the school's causes and picked up the first basket. The bidding began.

"Fifty cents!" was called out.

"Fifty cents." Repeated Mr. Wiger. "Do I hear a dollar?"

"One dollar!"

"I hear one dollar, do I hear one-fifty?"

Jake was amused as a farmer walked up and was awarded the basket for two dollars. His wife smiled at him with affection and they stood by to watch the next basket get auctioned.

The first baskets went quickly with husbands gaining their wives' handiwork, even though in good fun others tried to outbid them. Thane paid a handsome three dollars for Helma's basket, and she beamed with pride when he brought it back to her.

The mood seemed to change when it became known that the married ladies' baskets were gone. The baskets remaining belonged to the single women, the widows, and what some would call—the old maids.

The first one went quickly. The matching ribbon was such a give-away that Mr. Wiger good-naturedly chided the young couple for cheating. He held up the next one saying, "Now here's a lovely basket, no doubt prepared just for one of you bachelors to let you sample some good home cooking." He peeked under the cloth. "Mmm! Smells mighty good in there. Who will give a dollar?"

A motion from Mina made Jake aware that she was giving the young boy across the lawn from her a negative shake of her head. Jake chuckled. Seemed the young boy was getting hungry and was tired of waiting to make a bid for his food.

He kept his eye on Mina and saw her give the same negative shake over and over until Mr. Wiger lifted a large basket covered in a blue gingham cloth. An almost imperceptible nod from Mina to the young boy told Jake that this was the one. But when the lad didn't bid right away, Jake was puzzled. Mina was looking about the crowd as if she were seeking someone.

Does she have a beau? If so, where is he and why isn't he bidding?

A farmer in bib-overalls with whiskers touching his chest raised his hand at two dollars.

Mina pressed her lips together and kept up her search.

Next, a slick-haired salesman off the train put up his hand at three dollars.

Mina began nodding her head furiously at the boy. He called out, "Three dollars and fifty cents, Mr. Wiger!"

"Who is that? Ole Jasperson! What are you doing bidding?"

"No rule says I can't bid iffen I got the money, is there, Mr. Wiger?"

The auctioneer took off his hat, scratched his head and flipped his hat back on. "No, I guess not. Show me your money, boy."

Jake watched the boy run up and spread the money out in his hands. The auctioneer called out, "The bid is three dollars fifty; do I hear four?"

No one raised their hand or answered, so he handed the basket to Ole. "Little young for courtin', ain't ya, boy?"

Ole took off running with the basket, and the crowd waited to see which lady would claim it, but the boy headed to the trees and was out of sight. Jake kept his eye on Mina and saw her smile at the tall, blonde girl, who casually walked by her, saying something quietly as she did so.

They're up to something.

Jake crossed his arms and leaned against a tree. A few more baskets went without Mina seeming to care. Puzzled, Jake watched as Mina began looking into the trees where the boy had gone. She seemed to be getting agitated and then she stood to her feet, craning her neck into the woods as Mr. Wiger picked up the next basket.

"Why are you hiding out over here?"

The voice behind him startled Jake, and he turned to find Keane grinning behind him. "Ma's starting to set out our lunch over by the shade of the church. You coming?"

"Not yet. Go ahead without me."

Just then the tall, blonde hurried by with the boy named Ole by the hand. She walked swiftly to Mina, speaking to her in low tones.

"Is *that* Tuva Thomsen?" Keane's voice had an odd sound.

"Who?"

"It is! That's a girl I grew up with—Tuva Thomsen." He gave a low whistle. "She's not a kid anymore."

Jake watched the appreciation in Keane's eyes as he stared at his childhood friend, but Mr. Wiger's raised voice caught his attention.

"Four dollars! I have four dollars bid; do I hear four and fifty?"

"Your *mud girl* looks a little upset, Jake. Do you suppose it's her basket?"

There was a commotion as Ole Jasperson ran up to the auctioneer. "I bid five dollars, Mr. Wiger! Five dollars!" He held up the money.

"Ole, you can't bid again. You already got a basket, now go along with you."

Jake watched as Mina's eyes widened, and she looked frantically to the girl named Tuva for help.

"The bid is still at four dollars fifty cents; do I hear five?"

The salesman with his oiled down hair held up a hand.

"Five dollars! How about five and fifty? Do I hear five dollars fifty cents?"

"You going to rescue her, Jake?" Keane teased.

By Mina's reaction, it became obvious that the basket was hers. A group of the younger men had their heads together and Jake saw money changing hands. Then a young man in the center of the group called out, holding the money in the air, "Six dollars!"

The crowd stirred. The usual amount was three dollars at most. This was unheard of.

"Seven dollars!" The salesman called back.

Mr. Wiger was beside himself trying to keep the numbers straight. "Okay, we have a bid of seven, now do I hear—?"

"Ten dollars!"

The crowd gasped. Mina swung around as Jake stepped out of the shade.

Mr. Wiger stuttered out, "Ten! Ten! Is there—? Do I hear—? Sold!" He took out his handkerchief and mopped his forehead.

Jake pulled out his money and claimed the basket. He walked back to the shaded area of the tree and waited. Soon Mina approached.

"I think you have my basket there."

"Oh no! This is my basket. I paid good money for it." He smiled at her. "But I'd be willing to share it with you, if you please?"

Keane backed away from Jake and Mina. He was pleased for his friend, yet he felt a little uneasy. The men had been through such a terrible ordeal, that he didn't want to see Jake get hurt or suffer any more disappointments. Yet, what could he do?

"I guess, Lord Jesus, I have to learn to trust you in everything. Jake says to bring all our requests to you, so I request that you not let Jake get hurt

again. But that's just what I want. Only you know what is best for him...and for me."

Keane wasn't paying attention to where he was walking when he heard voices arguing. He rounded the corner of the hardware store and found Tuva and the boy Ole, both with a hand on the basket covered in blue gingham cloth.

"I told you I'd share it with you, Ole."

"Miss Mina said I could eat what's in there, and I'm going to, only I'm not going to eat it with no girl." He tugged again and freed the basket from her hands and took off at a run.

"Why, you little trouble-maker! Ole Jasperson!" Tuva put her hands on her hips in exasperation and swung around only to find herself face-to-face with Keane. They were about the same height, making Keane eye level with the icy blue eyes locked with his. He had seen that very same color in the waters off the coast of the Alaskan territory.

He realized he was staring.

"Hi Tuva."

"Keane."

She nodded and took a step as if to move away.

"You having a little trouble with the boy?"

"No. No trouble. Excuse me."

"Wait." Keane reached for her arm. "He bought your basket, didn't he?"

"Yes."

Keane chuckled. "Why?"

Color rose in Tuva's cheeks.

"I don't…I don't mean 'why would someone?' Keane stuttered. "What I mean is, why did he? He's a kid."

"Mother is waiting lunch for me."

"Tuva, are you mad at me?"

"No."

"Then why won't you look at me or talk to me?"

Tuva looked up and again Keane was struck by her eyes. He didn't know how long they stood that way, just looking at each other until Tuva pulled her arm away.

"I should go."

Suddenly Keane didn't want her to go. "No. I mean, why don't you eat with me? Ma fixed a big lunch and…"

A slight smirk crossed Tuva's face.

"What did I say?" Keane was puzzled.

"Do you think I need a *big* lunch?"

"What?" He smiled at her. "Tuva, are you laughing at me?" He was unexpectedly delighted. "Please, join us." He coaxed.

Tuva looked away and then back to him again. She nodded.

She's shy! And she's beautiful and funny and those eyes!

Keane took Tuva's hand and placed it in his arm as he led the way back to his parents.

Mina was thrilled to be lunching with Jake. Even though her plan almost went awry, it had worked out

in the end. She had told the boy Ole to wait until she
gave the okay to bid. She had been hoping that Keane
or Jake would show interest in either her basket or
Tuva's, but when she couldn't find them in the
crowd, she had to rely on the boy. She certainly
wasn't interested in dining with the others who were
bidding. But how was she to know that Ole wouldn't
be allowed to bid twice? But now, because she was
eating with Jake, she would finally be able to find out
the story of Keane Wheatly and where he had been
and who Jake really was.

"These are really good. Did you make them?"
Jake broke into her thoughts.

"Huh? Oh, the sandwiches. Yes, in fact Helma
Wheatly taught me how to bake bread properly. I
never did it right before. She's such a wonderful lady,
and she was so worried when Keane was away.
Where—?

"Aren't you going to have one?"

"What?

"Aren't you eating? I know I paid for the
basket, but I'm more than willing to share it with
you."

"Oh, I'm not very hungry. When did—?"

"Did you make the pie too? Apple, isn't it?
Looks delicious."

"Yes, yes I made the pie and the cookies and
the sandwiches and everything. Please, enjoy it. Now,
how did you and Keane—?"

"Are you sure you won't—?"

"Mr. Rodwell! I'm trying to carry on a
conversation with you."

"And I'm trying to eat."

Obviously stifling her exasperation, Mina folded her hands in her lap. "I'm sorry. Go ahead and eat, and we can talk when you are through."

Jake wiped his grin away with his napkin. He was amused that she was politely irritated with him. "Let's eat and enjoy the day together and we'll talk as we do so. Please, join me."

Mina took the sandwich he held out to her and reluctantly smiled. "I'm sorry. I can be so impatient at times, and my father says that I am much too curious for my own good. It's just that I've been worried about the Wheatlys for some time and wondered what had happened to their son."

Slowly Jake told their story. At times tears came to Mina's eyes, and even though he left out the most terrible things, he could tell that she knew there was more he didn't tell.

"So, that's what happened. Oh, those poor men! Why are people so cruel?"

Jake folded the napkin and returned it to the basket. "This world is full of sin, Mina. None of us can claim to be exempt from it. God says that even our righteousness is as filthy rags to him. But I am thankful that he cared enough to take our sin burden away at the cross. We are forgiven when we place our faith in what he did there. If I didn't know the Lord Jesus through all the years I was a prisoner, I don't think I would have come out of there alive to tell the story."

Mina had sat mesmerized through Jake's telling of Keane's story. "How long were you there, Jake? You told me about Keane. What about you?"

"My story began long before that. I grew up in a nice home with nice parents, but I was a rebel. I didn't like being told what to do, so I decided to go out on my own when I was sixteen. I only wrote to my folks when I needed some money to help get me out of trouble. They probably shouldn't have sent me any, but they cared, so they did. I changed my name, and got into all kinds of messes until I met Eva."

There was a change in Jake's voice as he talked about his wife. Mina watched him intently.

"She showed me what God's grace was all about. She turned my life around. I was going to reconnect with my parents and let them know I had changed, but then Eva got sick. She died and our baby boy died with her. After that, I just didn't care and that's when I was shanghaied and imprisoned on a ship for over three years. The rest you know."

As Jake talked, something started niggling at Mina's brain. Something he said was bothering her, but she wasn't sure what it was.

"Haven't you seen your folks since you were sixteen?"

"No, they—"

"Mina!" Mr. Prescott approached. "Oh, there you are. Hello, Mr. Rodwell. Mina, your mother isn't feeling well. She's asking for you."

Mina and Jake stood.

"Yes, Father." Mina turned to Jake. "Thank you for buying my basket and for the nice visit, Mr. Rodwell."

"You are most welcome, Miss Austinson/Asleson." Jake handed her the basket and nodded at her father.

Mina's father frowned at Mina as they walked back to the store. "Why does Mr. Rodwell call you that? Doesn't he know we don't own this store?"

"I don't know. I guess not. In fact, I'm not sure I ever told him our last name. No matter. How is mother? What's wrong?"

"It's that letter we got from your brother a while back. It's making her sick with worry."

Mina didn't have time to question her father any further as she made her way up the stairs and into her mother's bedroom.

"Mother, it's much too warm in here." Mina went to the closed windows and slid them open. The curtains moved from the slight breeze. "I declare it's hotter out there than in here. I think a storm may be coming by the looks of it." She turned to help loosen her mother's collar. "Let me get a cold cloth for your head. It hurts again, doesn't it?"

"You are so good, Mina. I wanted to stay and visit with the people, but I'm so worried about Thorpe."

"What is it? Where is he? Where has he been?"

Mrs. Prescott pointed to a letter on the table by the bedside. "You can read it."

With shaking fingers, Mina opened the letter and carefully read its contents. That niggling feeling she had while talking with Jake Rodwell came back to her. Thorpe said in the letter that he had been on a ship, but that now he was free and would finally reunite with his family. He wasn't sure where they were living now, but if they got the letter to send a telegram to Seattle, Washington.

Mina's brow puckered. She picked up the envelope and saw the letter was addressed to their old home in Ohio.

"Did you send a telegram, Mother?"

"Yes, your father sent one as soon as we heard. Oh, I shouldn't worry so, but there's always trouble when Thorpe is around. You hardly knew him, and he had no time for you. He was always in trouble with other boys, in trouble with the law, always wanting money. After he left home was when your father and I came to know the Lord. We never had a chance to tell Thorpe, and it's been years since we heard anything from him. We didn't even know if he was still alive, and now this. I fear something terrible will happen if he comes here, but he's our son. What else can we do?"

Mina swallowed just as a crack of lightening flashed out the window. She jumped. The wind was throwing branches and leaves at the open window, and she raced to close it. Her father ran in the room.

"We need to get downstairs."

twelve

The storm blew in so quickly that the picnickers had little time to gather their belongings and take shelter. Jake caught up with the Wheatlys as they were about to join others in the church. Already the branches of the elm trees were bent to the ground, and the makeshift tables that held the baskets were tipped on their sides.

Tuva had enjoyed the time with Keane and his folks. She and Helma were already good friends, but even though she had grown up with Keane and gone to school with him, he was still much of a stranger to her. As a schoolgirl she had been too bashful to join in schoolyard games. She stayed on the sidelines, tall and awkward among the other girls and tongue-tied around the boys. Keane was always nice to her, just as he was to all the others, but never seemed to really notice her. She, however, had always been aware of him.

Helma did most of the conversing during lunch with comments thrown in by Thane and Keane. Tuva had seen Helma's eyebrows rise when she walked over to them with her hand in Keane's arm, but the older woman did not embarrass her.

Tuva couldn't actually make herself believe that she was lunching with Keane and that he was looking at her and talking to her. And he *was* looking at her, staring so intently at times, so that she could hardly breathe.

The church was crowded with more people pushing their way in as the storm raged. Tuva stood at Keane's side, bumping against him as others jostled their way around them. His nearness was most distracting, especially when he gazed into her eyes the way he was at the moment.

"Your eyes...they're like the waters around the glaciers. They're beautiful."

Keane's words made her heart thump so loud she thought for sure he could hear it. Her voice was strangely high-pitched when she spoke.

"I have to find my family. They will be worried."

Keane answered without taking his eyes off her. "Maybe they're in here."

Tuva couldn't pull away from his gaze.

"I haven't seen them yet."

He smiled. "I suppose I should look." But as he turned to do so, he was pushed from behind. Tuva found herself encased in his arms.

"Sorry." He tried to back away only to be bumped forward again. "Sorry."

Tuva couldn't look at Keane. She pressed her lips tightly together and chanced a glance at him. She was unprepared to find his face so close to her own. She turned her head against his shoulder.

"Tuva? Are you laughing?"

Could this get any more embarrassing? At least we're not still gawking at each other.

"I have to go find my parents."

"Not in this, you're not. Just relax. They're sure to have found shelter too—oof!" Keane was pushed once again. "I am so sorry! You *are* laughing! Here I am, trying not to squash you, and you're laughing about it."

The room had grown dark with the storm and suddenly there was a flash of lightning followed almost immediately with rolling thunder and then a boom so deafening it shook the windows. Babies began crying and someone started praying. Keane's arms tightened around Tuva, and instinctively she held on to him. Then a steady tapping began, growing into what sounded to Tuva like hammers pounding on the roof.

"Hail!" someone shouted.

"The horses!" exclaimed another, but no move was made to leave the shelter of the building until the hail stopped.

Almost as quickly as the storm began, it moved on. The sun broke through and people began making their way out of the crowded church. Tuva slid her arms down to her sides as Keane was able to step away. She was even more embarrassed now and found that she couldn't meet his eyes.

Then she felt Keane's hand on her back once again. "Ma, I'm going to take Tuva to find her folks. I'll meet you at the wagon as soon as I can."

Keane directed her to follow the others out the door. The ground was covered in robin egg-size hail, and children were scooping up the ice balls and throwing them at each other as parents scolded.

"Watch your step."

Tuva was shaken, but not by the storm. Something happened in those moments she stood protected by Keane's arms. It was almost as if he was seeking protection in her as well. She had felt him shake and had heard his sharp intake of air. He had held her so tight that she could hardly breathe.

They had been making their way cautiously through the rain-soaked grass when Keane pulled Tuva to the side of the livery barn. He stood in front of her, not saying anything, just stared past her as if seeing something far away. Tuva waited.

"Tuva, I'm sorry about that. The storm brought back...it made me think of...You've heard what happened to me?" He looked directly at her.

Tuva nodded.

Keane released his breath. "I guess the storm made it all come back for a minute. I don't know how, but by the grace of God, Jake and I lived through it." He shook his head and smiled at her. "I just want you to know that I'd never take such liberties...I mean..."

"I know, Keane. I'm glad I was there."

They said nothing for a moment, just looked at each other. Tuva's gaze remained steady until Keane spoke again.

"I just want to make one thing perfectly clear." Keane's voice was serious, and Tuva tilted her head in question.

"You did laugh at me earlier when that big moose behind me kept shoving me into you."

Tuva's smile was mischievous. "I did."

Mina followed her mother back up the stairs to their living quarters. The storm had made them seek shelter in the small storeroom of the shop, and her father stepped outside to assess the damage to the town.

Mrs. Prescott put her hand to her forehead. "I think I'll lay down again and get some rest. I know I shouldn't worry about Thorpe." She smiled at Mina. "I'm sorry that I made you leave the picnic early for nothing."

"That's all right. I got in before the storm hit, so that was good."

Mina went to her own room, deep in thought. She *had* minded leaving early, but she didn't tell her mother that. She was enjoying Jake's company, and she felt he was having a good time with her as well. He had been through such a terrible ordeal, yet he still had a sense of humor and a love for the Lord that was unmistakable.

Mina saw that the rain had stopped so she went to the window and slid it open. She breathed deeply, loving the freshness of the air after the rain.

She looked out at the muddy streets and the scattered leaves, branches and debris. Two people over by the livery caught her eye and she peered closer out of curiosity.

Why, that's Tuva! And...Keane Wheatly!

She watched in fascination as the couple talked, and she blinked in astonishment when she saw Tuva smile at Keane and then take his arm and walk away. She wanted to run after Tuva and find out what had just happened. She straightened up with a smile on her face.

Jake was acutely aware of the growing attraction Keane had for Tuva Thomsen. He was close enough by them in the church to witness their embrace, and he had seen Keane's face and knew his friend was thinking of the storm out on the ocean. He was shaken himself.

Will it ever leave us? Will we relive it every time it storms?

He watched with interest as Keane and Tuva left the church, but he stayed with Helma and Thane and helped them get the horse hitched to the wagon. They were some of the fortunate ones who had stabled their horse during the picnic. Others who hadn't were now trying to calm frantic animals or worse, trying to catch a few who had bolted away.

He thought of Mina as he made his way through the mud. *Mud girl.* He had enjoyed the time with her during their lunch. She was a bit scatter-brained but charming all the same.

And lovely.

"That was some storm, wasn't it?" Keane appeared suddenly, shaking him out of his thoughts. "That's the way it can be here. The weather changes just like that." Keane snapped his fingers and grinned.

"Seems to me a lot of things can change, just like that." Jake snapped his fingers back at Keane and laughed, but there was a question in the look he gave him. Keane shrugged but avoided any answer as they worked together to brush the water from the wagon seat and spread it with the blanket Helma had packed for the picnic. After Thane and Helma were seated, the two men climbed on the back of the wagon and let their legs hang over the back. They could talk quietly without the older couple hearing them.

"That storm." Keane leaned to one side of the wagon to see Jake's face. "I felt like we were right back in that rowboat with those mountainous waves on either side of us. I think I'm still shaking a bit." He shook his head. "Did it bother you?"

Jake nodded. "It's only been a couple of months, so I'm not surprised, but I think…I hope it will get better with time." His grin was self-conscious. "I start to panic when your Ma sends me down to the root cellar to get something. Reminds me too much of the ship's hold." He didn't mention the irons that had chained him there, but Keane understood.

Keane took a deep breath. "Freedom! There's nothing better."

They rode in silence, both lost in their own thoughts of the past and the present. It was Jake who spoke again.

"So?"

Keane turned to him, puzzled. "So?"

"So you and the Norwegian goddess."

"The what?"

Jake waited and watched the color rise on Keane's neck.

"At least I didn't have to pay ten bucks to eat with her."

Both men broke out in laughter, but neither saw the look and the smile that passed between Thane and Helma.

thirteen

Keane was up earlier than the others the following morning. He tiptoed past Jake's bed, aware that Jake knew it but said nothing. He was out of the house and down the road in no time. He found the spot where he intended to wait and made himself comfortable. Now he could think.

Tuva was on his mind. What happened at the picnic yesterday was so unexpected that he was having trouble sorting it out. One thing he did know was that he had never really seen his neighbor and school mate before. But how could that be? She had always been a part of his life in one way or another. She visited their house but always to see his mother. He had never engaged her in conversation or even given her a thought.

He reminisced back to those days, which seemed so long ago now. The time he spent incarcerated on the ship was like a lifetime in comparison. But now, as he reflected back, he knew that he had been so self-centered before he had come to know Jesus as his savior that he thought little of anyone but himself. He had been dissatisfied with his life on the farm, longing for adventure and freedom to do as he pleased. The work on the railroad had given him some of that, even though it was hard work. He liked having money to spend on himself.

Keane rubbed the sleep out of his eyes. *"I was so selfish, Lord."* Then his freedom was taken from him, making him long for the home and farm he once knew. *Why is it always too late that we appreciate what we have?* If it hadn't been for Jake, he was sure he would have died out there.

Jake showed him a new life he could have in Christ. Keane smiled as he scanned the area around him. *"Thank you, Lord Jesus! Thank you for Jake, for my salvation, and..."* He paused in his thoughts then grinned. *"Lord, you know what I'm thinking, so I don't know why I hesitate to say it...thank you for Tuva."*

Keane's prayer was cut short when he saw a figure walking toward the elm tree. The sun hadn't appeared yet, but he could make out that it was a woman. He realized he was holding his breath as he waited. The woman easily swung herself onto the branch of the tree and sat still as if she too was waiting for something.

She didn't come every morning. Keane knew this because he had spent many mornings waiting and being disappointed when she didn't arrive. He never approached her. He never let her know he was there.

He just wanted to enjoy the moment with her. The sky was beginning to lighten and birds were beginning their songs now. He watched the figure in the tree in anticipation.

Then she began to sing.

Keane knew then. It was what he hoped. His heart was lifted in praise to the Lord along with the words of the hymn she sang. Just as the sun broke across the fields, her voice poured out the song:

> *Amazing grace! How sweet the sound*
> *That saved a wretch like me!*
> *I once was lost, but now am found;*
> *Was blind, but now I see.*

The last verse finished just as the sun filled the sky:

> *When we've been there ten thousand years,*
> *Bright shining as the sun,*
> *We've no less days to sing God's praise*
> *Than when we first begun.*

Keane listened, enraptured by the words and her voice. He knew this was a private time for her, and he knew he was intruding. He also guessed that because of her shyness, she wouldn't return in the mornings to sing if she found that someone was listening to her. He reluctantly watched her climb down and walk away.

His *bird girl*, as Jake teasingly called her, was Tuva Thomsen. Keane slowly rose from his hiding place and began walking back to the farm. He was overjoyed that they were one and the same person. He wanted to see Tuva again and to get to really know her.

I wonder why she isn't married.

Keane's thought stopped him and he swung around to look where Tuva had gone. He didn't like the thought of Tuva being married. He didn't like it one bit.

"Was she there?"

Jake's question caught Keane off guard later that day when they were working side by side chopping and stacking firewood. Keane had shared his *bird girl* sightings with Jake each time he heard her sing, but for some reason he was reluctant to say anything today. Everything was different now that he knew it was Tuva. He wanted to keep his thoughts on that to himself, but he also wanted to be truthful with his friend.

"She was." He went on to tell about the song and how the sun burst through at just the right moment. "I don't know how she does it, but it's like she knows which birds to harmonize with and how to time the sunrise. It feels like heaven opens up and the angels are singing with her."

"Do you know who she is yet?" The question was put innocently, but Keane couldn't help giving Jake a sharp look.

"You do, don't you!"

Now he'd done it. He looked away. "I think so." Keane swung the axe, splitting the log easily.

Jake said nothing for a moment, and Keane felt him watching him. To keep a secret from Jake seemed wrong. This was the man who had saved his life and had shown him a new life in Christ. If there was anyone who could give him advice, Jake would be it.

Keane leaned on the axe handle. "It's Tuva."

Jake let out a low whistle. "I see. What are you going to do about it?"

"Do? You think I should tell her I've been listening to her?"

Jake crossed his arms. "No. I think you should tell her you want to court her. You do, don't you?"

Keane sat down on a stump and squinted up at Jake. He didn't try denying that he wanted to court her because he did. "Is it too soon? I mean, I don't know that I'm ready. I'm still having nightmares and I'm terrified of lightning storms. And I wonder if it will ever go away."

Jake nodded in understanding. "I have the same fears, but like I said before, we now realize the brevity of our lives. God has brought us through a terrible time, but we're stronger for it. We've learned to depend on him to get us through each day. You know the Scripture we've been reading at night about the Apostle Paul in II Corinthians 11 and 12? Paul listed all the persecutions and perils he faced in his service for the Lord, and he went through much more than we have, yet he reminds us that the Lord said, 'My grace is sufficient for thee: for my strength is made perfect in weakness.' Then Paul concludes, 'Therefore I take pleasure in infirmities, in reproaches, in necessities, in persecutions, in distresses for Christ's sake: for when I am weak, then am I strong.'

"We are weak, Keane, because we're human, but our strength comes from the Lord. He'll get us through this time of adjustment, and I don't know how, but he'll use us for his glory because of it."

Keane nodded. "I got saved. That is something I will never forget. I'm just sorry it took such a drastic situation for me to see my need. When I was here on the farm, I wanted more adventure, but really, I had everything I needed. That's why I didn't feel any need for God. I never thought about death and what would happen to me."

Jake took out a handkerchief and wiped the moisture from his neck. "Your pastor asked if you and I would be willing to tell our story in church some time. Maybe we could help someone else see their need for Christ."

Keane smiled. "That's why everyone called you *Preacher*. You told us about God every chance you got." He took a deep breath. "I'm not so good at speaking, but I do want to share the Gospel with others. I guess I'd do it. And it might help some other young fellow appreciate what he has."

"Good. I think it would help us too, to get the story out, you know, to help us heal. Now back to Tuva."

Keane raised his eyebrows.

"You're drawn to her, so take some time to get to know her. Life goes on and finding the right person to share your life with can certainly make it more meaningful. My Eva was that to me."

"Would you marry again?"

Keane watched emotions cross over Jake's face. Jake took his time answering. "If I found the right person. It's heart breaking to say good-bye to someone you love, but it's a lonely life without someone to love."

"And…do you think you've found someone?" Keane's question was hesitant.

Jake laughed out loud. "Okay, you caught me. Yes, I find Mina quite interesting, and I do want to get to know her better. But I've got a lot of uncertainty ahead of me, not knowing if I'll stay here in Minnesota or where I'll end up. I like the farm and the work. It's satisfying in its way, but is it what I want to do with my life? I'm not sure yet."

"Have you thought about being a preacher, Preacher?"

Again Jake's answer was slow in coming. "It's something to pray about."

Word got out that the two men would be sharing their story in the Sunday service. There were several churches established in town, but the people filled the seats that Sunday in the Wheatly's church. Seemed like everyone wanted to hear about Keane Wheatly and his friend. Rumors had spread around, some saying Keane had been living it up but run out of money and had to finally come home. Some said the two were hiding out from the law, and some even said that the men had been prospecting in the Alaskan territory and struck it rich. Jake especially thought the last rumor the most interesting and guessed it was partly due to his paying off the Wheatly's bills.

Jake sat beside Keane near the front, waiting for the pastor's introduction after the service. He was having trouble concentrating on the sermon and he chided himself for that, but Keane's question about being a preacher kept coming to his mind.

"Is that the path for me, Lord? I want to tell others about you, but is that how I should be doing it?"

He was keenly aware of Mina and her parents sitting two rows behind him. He saw Keane glance over at Tuva who was holding a younger sibling on her lap. Both men were nervous about speaking, but even more so because of the presence of the two ladies. The pastor was closing in prayer, and Jake took time to pray that the words they spoke would be of benefit to the listeners.

Keane went first, and Jake prayed for his friend as he began. It was obvious he was unused to speaking before a group, but his intensity came through, and Jake found himself reliving the ordeal with him once again as he described the conditions in which they were incarcerated. Keane was direct and to the point.

"I grew up here. I went to church, but I didn't see why God mattered or what being a Christian meant. It wasn't important to me. But when I faced torment and torture, day after day, I found myself crying out to God, only I didn't know how to reach him. Jake came up with our escape plan, and I'll let him tell you that part, but Jake helped me escape more than slavery and more than death. He showed me the way to escape eternal death. He had no trouble convincing me that I was a sinner. I knew that. It was when he explained that it was my sin that caused Jesus Christ to go to the cross and shed his blood that it cut me to the quick. Believe me, I would have done anything to know I was going to heaven, but Jake told me verses that said I couldn't do enough even if I tried. I had to depend completely on what Jesus did for me. Not only did Jesus die for my sins, but he was buried, and he rose again. Only God could do that. I believed that day, and I've been thanking the Lord ever since for my salvation, for Jake, for life, for family, and for all the things I didn't think were all that important so long ago."

Keane had been holding both sides of the pulpit but now he pointed a finger at the people. "I don't know what's in your hearts. Only you and God know that. But I want you to think about your lives, especially you young men. Becoming a child of God is the most important thing you will ever have happen to you. You aren't a Christian because your parents are or because you sit in church every Sunday. Don't live your lives day after day without giving it a thought. Don't wait until you're facing death. Don't try to clean up your life before you dare approach the throne of Grace because you'll never get cleaned up by yourself. Trust in Christ's blood shed for your sins. Today!"

He turned to Jake and nodded, so Jake stood and changed places with Keane. As he stood in the pulpit, he saw women wiping at their eyes and some of the men looking at the floor. The younger listeners were staring at him with wide eyes. Keane's words had an effect.

They had decided ahead of time that Keane would begin and tell of his blunder in getting shanghaied and then describe what their lives had been like those painful years. They agreed not to be too graphic, but they did want the people to realize that these awful things were happening, not only to them, but also to many other unsuspecting men. Keane told of the death of young Tommy Rogers without going into too much detail, but enough for people to see that they faced death every day. Jake cleared his throat and began.

"It's only by the grace of God that I am able to stand here today and tell you our story. Escape was on everyone's mind, but after a while it began to seem impossible, especially after young Tommy's death. In some the hope of escape died. You could see it in their eyes, but it didn't die in Keane's eyes, and it didn't die in mine.

"Keane mentioned that the first mate was extremely cruel. The men called him Thor, god of thunder. He was the one responsible for Tommy Roger's death. He gave the orders. He was our master."

Jake went on to describe the night of the storm, the fire on the ship, the huge waves, and the wind. He could see the listeners were experiencing it with him. He told about the Rogers helping them, and how he and Keane learned that they were Tommy's parents. Again women were wiping the tears from their eyes.

"If you don't know the Lord Jesus Christ today, you're just like we were—slaves with no hope of escape. Your master isn't Thor, the god of thunder, but Satan, the god of this world. But there is a lifeboat available to you and someone to calm the sea for you. There is hope in Christ and in him alone. He died to be your savior. Believe him for your salvation and escape eternal death in the lake of fire."

Jake saw Mina looking at him with tears glistening in her eyes. She gave him a wobbly smile and he nodded in return. He took his seat beside Keane as the pastor returned to the pulpit once again and thanked them for sharing their experience with them. He prayed and the service was over.

Jake was kept busy shaking hands with people and was afraid he'd miss the chance to speak with Mina. Throughout his time in the pulpit, she had kept her eyes fastened on him, and he was aware of her in a way he hadn't been before.

She was waiting for him when he left the building.

"Jake...that was...I felt like I was there with you. I didn't begin to fathom all that you and Keane had gone through. I mean, you were on that ship for over three years!" Tears began to roll down her cheeks.

Jake took her arm and led her to the side of the church, away from curious onlookers. "It's okay. Please, don't cry, Mina. It's over." He found that he wanted to take her in his arms and comfort her, but this wasn't the time and it certainly wasn't the place.

"Oh, I'm so sorry! Here I am blubbering away. I don't know what you must think of me."

"I think you're a caring, loving person, whom I would like to get to know better. May I call on you, Miss Austinson-Asleson?"

For a moment Mina appeared to be speechless as she stared at Jake then she stuttered, "Uh...yes. Yes, please do! I mean, that would be lovely." Then she frowned. "You know that's not my name, don't you? It's—"

"Mina!"

"Oh, dear, that's Mother calling me." She looked up at Jake again. "You will come then?"

Jake smiled. "I will come calling."

She moved to go then turned back. "Soon?"

Jake laughed. "Soon, Miss Mina. Very soon."

She gave him a brilliant smile. "Bye, Jake."

"Bye."

He watched her join her parents. *Eva would have liked her.* The thought made him smile. Eva would have wanted him to move on with his life, and with Mina's help, maybe he could.

Keane was aware of Tuva's attention on him while he spoke. It should have made him more nervous, but somehow it calmed him. Even though he didn't make direct eye contact with her, he felt that he was speaking to her as he told his story. It was tough to relate the horrors they had gone through, but Keane hoped and prayed that by doing so it might lead someone to Christ.

He was self-conscious, visiting with people afterward and receiving their thanks and their sympathies. It was Tuva he wanted to talk to, but she was surrounded by her younger siblings, who seemed to be left in her care while her parents did some visiting. He worked his way over to her and scooped up the toddler who was about to pitch head first into a mud puddle.

"Hey, little guy! I don't think your big sister wants you to splatter mud on her pretty skirt."

Tuva smiled at Keane and at her brother, who was staring in astonishment at the man who was holding him. But it was only a moment that he stared. In the next instant he screwed up his face and let out a howl of panic that brought his mother running.

"Goodness! Such a fuss!" Mrs. Thomsen took her son from Keane's arms. "Hello, Keane. Thank you for sharing your story today, and thank the good Lord you made it home again."

"Yes, ma'am. Thank you, ma'am." Keane watched in amazement as the little boy immediately stopped his ruckus once he was in his mother's arms. The toddler peeked at him over her shoulder and wiggled his chubby fingers at him.

"Viktor isn't used to you, that's why he cried." Tuva tried to explain.

"I can't say that I blame him. I did sneak up on him from behind." Keane laughed. He saw that the Thomsens were gathering their brood into their wagon and he knew he was running out of time. "Tuva, I—"

"Sometimes I like to walk home after church." Tuva's statement was quiet and she wasn't looking at him, so it took Keane a moment to understand.

"Oh...I see...would you be agreeable with me walking with you?" He saw a blush creep up her face, but she only nodded, again without looking at him. "Uh, should I ask your father?"

"Yes, I think so."

Keane wasn't sure what he said to Mr. Thomsen nor what he told his folks, all he knew was that after the commotion of wagons and buggies leaving town, he found himself keeping pace with Tuva's long strides. He glanced at her and saw that she was looking straight ahead as she walked.

"Let's slow down a bit, huh?"

Tuva immediately slowed her pace. "I'm sorry. I'm so used to having to get places in a hurry."

Keane nodded. "Me too, but I don't really want to get anywhere right now. I just want a chance to talk with you and spend some time with you."

Silence.

"So, shall we talk?" Keane asked.

Tuva nodded.

Keane stopped walking, causing Tuva to halt and look at him. "You're shy. I guess I'm a little nervous about this too." He held up a hand. "Not because I'm nervous about *you*, it's only because I've never done anything like this before, and..." He stopped talking and looked at her bowed head.

"Tuva! Are you laughing at me again?"

She raised her head to meet his eyes, and he could see her struggling not to smile.

"You have beautiful eyes."

The words were out of his mouth, surprising him as much as her. Her expression changed in an instant and she stared at him, but now that he'd started he couldn't seem to stop. "And your braids...you're like a Nordic princess."

She turned from him then and started walking again. Keane quickened his pace to catch up. "Tuva?"

He was afraid he'd scared her away but then she smiled at him, and when Keane reached for her hand, she took his. Her words were soft, but Keane heard them.

"Thank you, Keane."

fourteen

It took some doing, but Thorpe learned that the two men had transferred to a train heading into Minnesota. This new conductor, however, was not so easily bribed as the previous one.

"No matter to me how much money you're offering, mister. Ain't none of my affair, and I aim to keep it that way."

Thorpe kept his temper under control while he stared out the window, even though his mood was as dark as his hair. His men were rattling off the names of small towns in the area.

"There's Hawley, Lake Park, Hitterdal, Ulen, Syre, Twin Valley…"

"Hey, mister. Maybe I can be of service."

Thorpe felt a tap on his shoulder. He turned slightly to see a man craning his neck to smile at him. He nodded to one of his men to vacate his seat so the stranger could face him. The man was in a dusty business suit and carried a case with him. A salesman, no doubt. A salesman who was ready to make a sale.

"Heard you asking about the whereabouts of a couple of men. I'm in farm equipment." He pointed to his case. "I make a circuit of the towns 'round about and visit the stores, but I also get out to the farms and speak directly to the farmers, so maybe you give me a name, and I might know which town you need." He fingered the lapel on his jacket and kept a smile on his face while he waited for a reply.

Thorpe looked the man up and down, knowing that he was making him nervous. Control was important. His first instinct was to take the smooth-talking peddler by the throat and force information out of him, but he couldn't afford to draw attention to himself that way. He gave a slight nod of his head to his man who slipped a couple of bills into the salesman's hand.

"Wheatly and Rodwell. Over two months ago."

The man pocketed the bills and licked his lips. "Let's see. Yes, the name Wheatly is familiar. There's a Thane Wheatly not far from Ulen. Yes sir, I bet he's your man. The other name though..." He shook his head. "I don't recall that one."

Thorpe nodded and turned back to the window.

"You need anything else, mister? You planning on farming? I got every—"

He got no further. Thorpe's man picked him up by the collar and gave him a shove, nearly knocking him off his feet. The man grabbed his case and scurried away into another car.

Thorpe's eyes never left the scenery out the window.

"We're getting off in Ulen."

The men did not get off at the same time, nor did they all go in the same direction. Thorpe made his way to the hotel, paying no attention to where the others went.

City Hotel. They think this is a city?

His expression did not give away his thoughts as he registered and went to his room. His men would make inquiries and scout out the town and get back to him. For now he would wait. He sighed as he threw his hat on the quilt-covered bed. He fingered the brass bedpost and eyed in disdain the sparsely furnished room. The mirror over the washstand was tilted too low for him to even see his face, so he bent down to run his fingers through his black hair. He would need a shave soon. Even on the ship, he kept his face free of whiskers. It was another way to show the men that he had a freedom they did not have.

He unbuttoned his coat and slipped his right arm out of it then carefully slid the sleeve off his left arm. He rolled up his shirt sleeve and looked at the scars remaining from the burns. Anger made him clench his teeth, and when he looked up into the mirror again, he could see the anger reflected in his eyes.

He made his way to the window and looked down at the street below. Puddles were everywhere testifying to rain the previous day, yet business appeared to be going on despite them. Whatever business went on in this place.

Thorpe raised his gaze to the fields beyond the town. The grain in the unending fields waved in the wind, reminding him of the ocean. It had a beauty all its own, which Thorpe had to appreciate, but he could never be satisfied here. He had to be in a big city where the action was, where there was money to be made, where he had power.

He turned back to the street below and watched as two women met on the boardwalk across the street. The shorter one was very animated as she talked to the taller one. Thorpe squinted and moved closer to the glass pane. In Seattle, fashion was important and the ladies he entertained wore the latest styles. Huge, elaborate hats were especially the rage. Thorpe allowed himself a smile as he studied the Minnesota ladies. Both wore dresses that he assumed were considered serviceable. *Probably the typical farm girls.* The shorter, dark-haired one was a bit fancier with some lace and ribbons, but the tall one was dressed very plain. She didn't even wear a hat or bonnet, but as she turned so that Thorpe could see her face, his smile disappeared and he simply stared. *No wonder she doesn't wear a hat. That blonde braid is like a crown.*

She was quite beautiful. Thorpe was enjoying the view, and he smiled again when he saw the blonde roll her eyes at something the dark-haired girl said to her. The shorter girl shook her finger at her friend and then gave her a little wave and turned to cross the street.

Now Thorpe had a good look at her as well, and something struck him. She was also a beauty, and to his experienced eye, seemed completely unaware of it. She smiled and waved at another person walking by then glanced upward, and for some reason he ducked back from the window. He had seen her clearly and he liked what he saw, but he would introduce himself to her on his terms.

Never expected this! Could be I'll have to spend a bit more time here.

Mina was busy with her thoughts as she walked back to the store. Tuva could deny it all she wished, but Mina knew she had fallen for Keane Wheatly. It took some doing to get the information out of the shy girl, but Mina coaxed and prodded until she had the whole story about the picnic and the storm and the church. However, when she asked what they talked about on their walk, Tuva clammed up.

Then Tuva turned the tables on Mina and wanted to know about her lunch with Jake. But Mina was evasive.

"I do like him, and I loved hearing him speak in church. Didn't he and Keane do such a good job? If there was anyone there who didn't feel the need to know the Lord Jesus, I don't know who it would be! The terrible things they went through!" As usual, Mina emphasized her words with hand gestures, but Tuva caught her hands and held them down.

"How do you really feel about him?" The question was serious.

Mina stammered, "I...I...Oh, Tuva! I care so very much, but..."

"What's wrong?"

Suddenly Mina shrugged. "Oh, it's probably nothing, at least nothing for you to worry about." She pointed her finger at Tuva. "I need to get back now. My folks are waiting. Bye." She waved her hand and crossed the street, waving at another couple before heading to the store.

What she couldn't tell Tuva, what she hadn't told her parents, and what she really didn't want to believe was that she had a suspicion about Jake.

Father was getting ready to close for the day, so Mina went for the broom and helped him finish cleaning up. Before long they were ready to go upstairs where her mother had supper waiting for them. Mina was quiet during the meal and knew her parents were wondering why, but she waited until they were finished and had put away the cleaned dishes. Her mother finally put forth a question.

"Wilhelmina, something's bothering you. Do you want to talk about it?"

Mina took a deep breath and nodded. "Could I see that letter from Thorpe again first, please?"

"The letter? Why? Mina, do you know something about Thorpe?"

Mina gave a short negative shake of her head. "I just want to see if I read it right."

Her mother gave her an odd look, but she went to her room to retrieve the letter. She handed it to Mina, who quickly opened it and scanned the contents. Mrs. Prescott reached for her husband's hand, concern wrinkling her brow. "Mina, what is going on?"

Mina took a moment to look at one parent then the other before she blurted out, "I think Thorpe is here already."

What do you mean he's here already? Have you seen him? Has he spoken to you?"

"No. Well, maybe. I'm not sure."

"Wilhelmina! Please explain yourself."

Mina paced in front of her parents while she tried to think what the letter from her brother said. He was on a ship. Jake had been on a ship. He was free. That could mean he had been a prisoner like Jake was. Jake had changed his name. Jake's family sent him money. Jake left home when he was sixteen. It all seemed to add up, so she relayed her thoughts to her parents.

"Don't you see? It could be that Jake Rodwell is really Thorpe. He must still think we're in Ohio, and he doesn't know our last name." She turned to her father. "You heard him. He calls me Mina Austinson/Asleson because he thinks we own this store and that one of those has to be my last name."

Her father shook his head. "I didn't see any resemblance to Thorpe in him. Sure, it's been fifteen years, but wouldn't we recognize our own son?" He asked his wife.

Mrs. Prescott rubbed her fingers on her temples as if trying to relieve pain. "I admit there are some similarities in their stories, but I can't believe my son would change so much that I wouldn't know him! But say he has changed." She turned to her husband. "We haven't changed so much that he wouldn't know us, have we?"

Mr. Prescott slid his arm around her. "You haven't changed at all, my dear. But think. A sixteen-year-old boy would have an entirely different perspective than a thirty-one year old man." He shook his head as he looked at Mina. "I don't know what to think. I suppose you know that Jake asked my permission to call on you?"

Mrs. Prescott put her hand over her mouth as she stared at Mina.

Mina closed her eyes for a moment before facing her parents. "I have to find out the truth."

"Not you, Mina. For now, I think it best that you not see Jake Rodwell until we get this straightened out." He looked at his wife again. "Could that young man who spoke so eloquently in church really be our son?"

"Oh, wouldn't that be wonderful!"

Mina slipped out of the room to the privacy of her bedroom where she allowed the tears she had been holding back to slide down her face. Yes, it would be wonderful for them as a family to have Thorpe so changed, but for herself it was so very painful. She liked Jake. She admitted that she liked him very much and had begun to think he cared for her too, but now that would be impossible. No matter what her parents thought, Mina was convinced that Jake Rodwell was really her brother. According to her parents, Thorpe had been in trouble since he was a boy, but the experience of being shanghaied must have changed him considerably because Jake was the kindest, most thoughtful, respectful, God-fearing man she knew. She had to find a way to get him to admit who he really was.

She frowned. Maybe he had to change his name because the law is looking for a man named Thorpe Prescott. Maybe his past deeds are still waiting to catch up to him and maybe he's here, using the Wheatly farm as a hideout. Maybe he never really was on that ship and that was just a story he's using. Maybe he's just really good at pretending to be so wonderful.

Brother or not, she needed the truth, and she was going to get it.

The next day Mina was off in the buggy with her mother's blessing. She felt a prick of her conscience at telling her mother she was going to visit Tuva when she really was on her way to the Wheatlys. Father had expressly said to stay away from Jake Rodwell until they knew whether he was Thorpe or not, but Mina's logic was that by going there, she would find out the truth.

It turned out to be a bad time to come. All the men were out in the field, and Mina stopped the horse to watch them cutting grain with the binder. Jake was shocking the bundles, and he moved swiftly behind Keane and his father, taking the bundles and stacking them vertically so they could dry and to keep the rain from soaking into them. Mina watched for a long time, following Jake's every move. He was working hard and he seemed to be enjoying himself. Mina heard him raise his voice in song.

Could her wicked brother really have changed so much? Is Jake pretending or is he genuine?

"I hope...I pray, Lord, that he's not Thorpe! I mean, if he is, I'm glad to see that he's changed, but...but I wish he was just Jake."

Mina didn't know what she should pray for, but she knew God understood. She turned the horse and buggy around to head back to town, more puzzled than before.

"Hey, isn't that your *mud girl*?" Keane pointed to the buggy headed away. "Wonder why she didn't stop?"

Thane pulled up the horse next to his son. "Mud girl?"

Keane laughed at Jake's sideways glance as he answered his father. "It's Mina from the store in town. The first time we met her she was covered in mud." He went on to explain.

Thane chuckled. "She seems to get into predicaments, that's for sure. Ole Sorenson got some chewing tobacco from the store one day, and she accidentally filled his pouch with black pepper. I guess she was daydreaming or something, but when Ole put a pinch in his jaw, he sure got a jolt!"

Jake grinned as the men laughed. He looked after the departing buggy and wished that Mina had stopped. He turned when he heard Helma coming with their lunch.

"Is that Mina? Oh, call to her, would you? I have some things to return to her."

Jake was glad to oblige. He took off on a run. "Mina! Mina!"

Mina drew in the horse and turned, surprise on her face, as Jake ran across the field to her. He wasn't even out of breath when he stopped beside the buggy.

"Where are you going in such a hurry? Weren't you going to stop and say hello?" He smiled at her.

"You...you were all so busy. I didn't want to bother you."

"Come, bother us. Helma says she has some things to return to you, and we're about to have lunch. I bet she'd share some with you and you wouldn't even have to bid for it."

Mina smiled, but Jake saw her hesitate. "Anything wrong, Mina?"

"No, nothing." She glanced up at the others in the field. "Are you sure I won't be in the way?"

"Of course, I'm sure." Jake took the horse's bridle and helped turn him again and walked along until they got close to the others. "I think we can walk in from here." He held out his hand to help her down, aware that he was dirty and sweaty and in no condition to be near her. "You'll have to excuse my appearance."

"You look fine." She smiled, but Jake noticed that she seemed preoccupied. They took a few steps, until Mina stopped abruptly. Jake halted and turned to her.

"What is it?"

"Jake, do you...do you know anyone named...Thorpe?" Mina watched him with wide eyes.

Jake's reaction was so swift, Mina was almost knocked over when he took hold of her shoulders and stared at her. "Have you talked to someone? Where did you hear that name?"

Mina was stuttering, trying to answer when Keane joined them, concern on his face. "What's the matter? Jake, what's wrong?"

But Jake was concentrating on Mina. "Mina, where did you hear that name? It's important!"

Mina pulled free from Jake and backed away. "I…I have to go." She turned and ran. Jake was about to follow, but Keane held him back.

"What name, Jake? What's the matter with Mina?"

Jake watched Mina slap the reins on the horse, turn, and take off. He wanted to run after her and find out more, but something wasn't right. She was afraid. Afraid of *him*. He faced Keane and spoke quietly so that the Wheatlys couldn't hear.

"She asked if I know someone named Thorpe."

Keane's sharp gasp and clenched fists were his immediate reaction. "Is he here? He wouldn't be! Why would he come all this way for us?"

"I don't know. I don't even know if he is here, but why else would she ask that? And why did she take off so suddenly?" Jake rubbed the back of his neck as he studied the ground. "We can't be sure, but we better be prepared." He looked over at Thane and Helma who were watching them and waiting for them to return. "And we can't let him near your folks. Above all, we have to protect them." He drew in a shaky breath. "We have to tell them, Keane. That's the only way they will be safe. They can be on guard. Maybe…maybe we should leave…"

"Or we could send my folks away, out of danger. We could—"

"What's wrong, boys?" Thane had walked up behind them without them hearing him. "Why would we be in danger?"

"Pa!" Keane looked to Jake for help.

"Tell us, son. Tell us both." He motioned for Helma to join them.

Reluctantly, Keane told what they knew, what they suspected, and what they feared. He pleaded with his parents to seek refuge away from the area, so that they would not fall into whatever plan Thorpe had for them.

"No." Thane was vehement and Helma nodded in agreement. "Your Ma and I lost you once. We'll not hide away and let you face this man alone. Now, let's think this thing through. We don't know for sure that this is the man from your ship. All we have is a name. But let's prepare as if he is here and is going to cause trouble for you. I think it best if I notify the sheriff and some of the neighbors."

Jake had remained silent, but he spoke now. "He won't be alone. Thor—Thorpe will have men with him. If he is here."

"Well, maybe that's the first thing we need to find out—if he's here." Thane unhitched the horse. "Let's head back to the house and talk this through. I don't like you two being out in the open."

Helma was fighting back tears. "No one's taking you boys anywhere!"

fifteen

If there was one thing good Thorpe could say about the town of Ulen it was the cooking. The hotel didn't offer a choice of menu foods—the customer got what was cooked that day, but what was served was to his liking and plenty of it. Even though the captain and his men were served much better food than the enslaved sailors aboard ship, still, it couldn't compare to home cooking like this. He sat alone at a table, noting that his men came and went without acknowledging him, as were his instructions.

It was the previous evening in his room that he got reports from the men. There was indeed a farmer named Thane Wheatly and he had a son named Keane. Thorpe had not known what Wheatly's first name was until hearing the Rogers use it. On the ship he had only the name Wheatly to go by and had no need to know anything else about the man who was nothing but a slave to him. Word was that Keane had been away for over two years and had only returned a few months ago. That fit.

"The preacher is here too. Came with Wheatly and is staying on the farm. Name's Jake Rodwell, just as you said."

Thorpe ran his hand over his burn scarred arm and felt the scarred tightness on his side. He had them now! It didn't matter to him that others had escaped the ship. It was these two who planned their escape and took the rowboat. It didn't matter that lightning started the fire. In Thorpe's mind, these men were responsible for his burns.

"Are we taking them back on the train?"

Thorpe stared at the floor as he thought. "No. I want to take care of it here. When it's done, I'm going to travel a bit and you can come with me or go back. It's up to you."

One of the men spoke up. "Pay's good with you, Thorpe. I'll stay on."

The other two agreed.

"There will be extra for you when this job's done." Thorpe accepted their allegiance with a nod. He turned to one of the men. "Send a telegram to Seattle to see if I've had any messages and have them forwarded here in your name." He looked at the others. "Find a private place we can take Wheatly and Rodwell. I want to have a talk with them first. We'll go in tomorrow night, so get some rest." He walked to the window and looked out. "I think I'll take a walk tomorrow and take in the sights of this town."

The men seemed puzzled by his comment, but they said nothing as they filed out of the room.

The next morning Thorpe finished his breakfast and strode out of the hotel. He paused on the boardwalk to take stock of his surroundings. Besides the hotel and the railroad, there were the typical businesses: a post office, a couple general stores, a hardware store, some grain elevators, a blacksmith, and a livery and harness shop. A few residences were plotted behind the businesses, and churches appeared on corners.

He started walking, taking his time to look in windows, tipping his hat to women who passed by. He was looking for the two young ladies he had seen the previous day from his window, as well as for others like them. He slowed his step when he saw the dark-haired girl exit a store. He heard her call something over her shoulder to someone inside.

"I'll be back this afternoon, Father, in time to help unload the new merchandise."

Thorpe glanced up at the sign above the doorway to the store. "Austinson & Asleson General Store". *Wonder which one she is.*

He followed her at a leisurely pace as she made her way to the post office. She was back out in a few moments and had a frown on her face that he found enchanting. He was about to approach her when he heard a voice from behind him.

"Mina!"

The dark-haired girl turned toward the voice and her frown was replaced with a smile. Thorpe leaned against a post and pretended disinterest as the tall, blonde girl from the day before approached the other.

"Mina, I'm glad I caught you."

"Hi, Tuva."

The girl named Tuva answered, but her voice was too quiet for Thorpe to hear the words. Mina's voice was clear though.

"Are you sure Keane didn't say anything to you about Jake?"

Thorpe's head jerked, but he willed himself to stay still. He listened intently while the shorter girl continued.

"Well, I've decided to go and have a talk with him. I ran away like a scared rabbit yesterday, so he must be wondering about me. And I need you to go with me." Her tone changed to cajoling. "You'll get to see Keane again."

The coaxing must have worked because Thorpe saw the taller girl nod her head and sigh. "I don't know why I let you talk me into things, Mina."

"I can't explain right now, but I really do need you to be with me." She looked down at a paper in her hand. "I have to finish these errands for my folks then I'll meet you at the livery in about fifteen minutes."

They parted ways and Thorpe sauntered off, not worried about keeping track of their whereabouts since he knew the girls were meeting again at the livery. *And they'll take me right to Wheatly and Rodwell.* He needed to gather his men.

He caught sight of one of the men and gave him a nod. The man made his way to where Thorpe waited.

"Get the others together and get horses. Meet me behind the hotel as soon as you're ready."

The man nodded and slipped a paper in Thorpe's hand and moved on. Thorpe looked down at the note and saw it was a telegram. He tucked it in his breast pocket and made his way to the hotel and to his room.

He was getting excited now, but it didn't show. Even when he was alone in his room, he kept his features from showing what was going on inside him. His heart was beginning to thump harder and a small bead of sweat formed on his upper lip. It was always this way when he was about to exert his power over someone.

He took out his pistol and checked it over then tapped his booted leg to make sure his knife was in place. His men would be heavily armed as well, but not so that anyone would take notice. The only difficulty they might face is how to follow the two women without being seen. This open prairie and farm fields left little to hide behind. The men knew the location of the Wheatly farm and could get there by separate ways, but he needed to follow the girls in case Wheatly and Rodwell were somewhere else today.

Feeling confident that he was prepared, Thorpe left the hotel and casually walked down the boardwalk. He'd make his way behind the hotel when the girls left town. For now he'd just take it easy, so he found a bench out in front of one of the stores and sat, adjusting his hat forward over his face as if napping.

A moment later he felt the presence of someone and he lifted his chin. It was one of his men, standing beside the bench, not looking at him.

"Sorry, Thorpe. Can't find Cal anywhere."

Thorpe restrained his anger, but his voice betrayed him. "We'll go without him."

"Yes, boss."

The man walked away. Thorpe forced himself to relax again, but a feminine voice caught him off guard.

"Excuse me. Did I hear that you are looking for Thorpe? Thorpe Prescott?"

Stunned, he turned to the voice, but was careful not to reveal his surprise. "Hello. What was that you asked?" He rose to his feet and took off his hat.

The dark-haired girl was obviously frightened. "I'm sorry. I didn't mean to listen, but I thought that man said you were looking for someone named Thorpe. Would that be Thorpe Prescott?"

Thorpe had no idea how to answer the girl. *He* was Thorpe Prescott! Was there someone else using his name? He decided to play along.

"Yes, as a matter of fact I am looking for him. Do you know where I might find him?"

He watched the color leave her face and when she swayed, he reached out to steady her.

"Is he…is he in trouble? Are you a lawman?"

Her questions were even more confusing, but he decided to try reassuring her. "No, miss. It's nothing like that. He's just a friend of mine and I was passing through here and thought I'd pay my respects. Do you know where I might find him?"

"Um…no. No, excuse me, please. I have to go." She pulled her arm away and hurried off down the boardwalk, leaving Thorpe staring after her.

Who is using my name? What is going on here?

He was uneasy. Somehow Wheatly and Rodwell had to be responsible for this. He didn't know what this was about, but the answer had to be with that girl. He'd stick to the plan of following her even if that meant she was going to warn the person using his name or that she was going to the Wheatly farm. Either way, she was the key. He left the boardwalk and made his way to the back of the hotel.

"Still no sign of Cal, boss. I don't like it. He's usually dependable."

Thorpe was still mulling over the situation he found himself in and paid little attention to the man.

"You make your way to the Wheatly farm and stay out of sight. You other two—where's Cal?"

The men looked at one another in puzzlement before one of them answered. "Told you we couldn't find him."

"He's fired then." Thorpe was angry now. He didn't like losing control, but the girl's questions had unsettled him. He turned to his man. "Follow me, but keep way back. I don't know for sure the two women will go to the Wheatlys." He didn't say anything about what the dark-haired girl had asked him.

"Boss, did you read the telegram?"

"The what?"

The man scowled. "The telegram I gave you."

"No time for that now. You two take off. Those women are getting ready to leave." He turned back to the man who questioned him. "Did you find a place we can take Wheatly and Rodwell?"

"Figured the barn would do. The old couple should give us no trouble. It would just be the two women then." He left the statement hanging.

"When does the train leave?"

"About eight tonight."

"Should give us plenty of time if things go right." Thorpe watched the buggy disappear down the road. "Okay, I'm going now. Leave plenty of space between us, but close enough you can see if I turn off to follow them somewhere else."

"Got it."

Thorpe mounted the horse and walked him away. He felt in the rifle scabbard for the whip his man had put there. His plan was underway and it brought back the excitement he had felt in the hotel room. Those two men were going to pay for escaping. They'd get the whipping they deserved and then they'd be killed. But they were going to know who was doing it and why first. He moved his left arm and felt the tightened skin there. *Oh, they'll pay!*

"Will you for heaven's sake slow down, Mina! And I swear if you don't tell me what's bothering you, I'm jumping out and walking home."

Mina pulled on the reins and handed them over to Tuva. "You take them. I'm sorry! Oh, Tuva! I'm so scared."

Tuva called to the horse. "Whoa, Duncan! What has gotten into you, Mina? Why are you scared? What's happened?"

But Mina pointed to the horse. "We can't stop! We have to get there to warn him!"

"Warn who? About what?"

Mina grabbed Tuva's arm. "You just keep driving and I'll try to explain."

Tuva frowned but slapped the reins, putting the horse back in motion. "Now talk!"

Mina gripped the edge of the seat with one hand and with the other she wiped back tears that started streaming down her face. "I had so hoped..." she began. She shook her head as if to dispel whatever thoughts she'd had and continued. "It's Jake. He's been lying to us. His name is not Jake Rodwell."

Tuva jerked her head to stare at Mina, but she said nothing.

"He's really...he's...oh, Tuva! He's my brother!"

"Your *brother*!"

Mina found a handkerchief and wiped at her face. She nodded her head. "I suspected it, and when I mentioned the name Thorpe to him, he got awfully upset, so I knew it was him."

"What does that mean? I don't understand you."

"My brother's name is Thorpe. I don't remember him because I was so little when he left home, but my parents say that he's been in all kinds of trouble, and that he lies and he steals and I don't know what all, but I just can't believe that Jake is like that, but he must be since he's Thorpe, but maybe he's changed now. I can only hope so, but that man in town is looking for him, and that can't be good, because if he is in trouble with the law, that man might be here to arrest him, and I have to warn him."

Mina paused for breath and finally noticed that Tuva had stopped Duncan and was staring at her.

"No! Keep going! We have to warn him!"

But Tuva shook her head. "Just hold on a minute. You're not making any sense, and I'm not going to go barging into the Wheatlys until I know what exactly is happening here. Now start again."

Mina was clearly frustrated at the delay, but she took a deep breath and started again. "Jake is my brother Thorpe. I don't know why he's been lying, but I think he must be hiding from the law. There is a man in town who is looking for him, and I don't care if Thorpe did something bad or not, he's my brother, and I'm going to warn him to leave before the man finds him." Defiance sparked in her eyes as she reached for the reins in Tuva's hands, but Tuva pulled them away from her.

"Okay. I'll get us to the Wheatlys. You're in no condition to handle Duncan right now." She again slapped the reins. "But once we get there, you better make more sense than you are now or they're all going to think you've gone loco."

Mina said nothing in reply as she wondered herself if her actions were crazy. But what else could she do? If Thorpe was truly in trouble, she had a responsibility as his sister to help him, didn't she? On the other hand, she couldn't deny that her feelings for the man called Jake ran deeper than what a sister would feel for her brother. She felt tears prick her eyes again.

"Lord Jesus, I'm so mixed up! Help me sort this out!"

Tuva slowed Duncan as they pulled into the Wheatly's farmyard. She stopped him and set the brake, but Mina jumped down before the buggy even stopped swaying and ran to the door. Tuva quickly followed, shaking her head as Mina pounded with her fist on the door.

"Mina! Settle down! You're going to frighten them."

There was no response from the house, so Mina called out, "Helma! Keane! Jake! Is anyone home?"

"Mina?"

The girls turned to Jake as he walked from the barn. He carried a rifle at his side.

"Oh, Jake!" Mina ran to him with Tuva on her heels. "Jake, someone is looking for you! He knows you're here and he knows...he knows who you really are." Mina flung her arms around him. "I had to warn you...no matter what you've done."

Jake looked over Mina's head at Tuva, the frown on his face clearly showing his puzzlement. "What do you mean?" He questioned Tuva. "What's she talking about?"

Tuva's shrug and shake of her head told him nothing, but Mina pushed away and wiped at her eyes. "You can admit it to me, Jake. I know who you are."

Jake looked down at her and shook his head in bewilderment. "What—?"

"You're Thorpe, aren't you?"

Jake became very still. "I don't understand. How do you know Thorpe Prescott? That is who you're talking about, right? Thorpe Prescott? How do you know him?" he repeated, his question insistent.

Mina straightened up away from him. "I'm Wilhelmina Prescott, your sister."

Jake stared at her. "*My* sister! You think *I'm* Thorpe? You're his sister?"

Mina's voice was pleading. "Oh, Jake, you don't have to lie anymore, but you do have to get out of here. There's a man looking for you. I don't care what you've done—"

"What man? Where did you see him? What did he say to you?"

"Jake! It doesn't matter. Just leave, please! I don't want Father and Mother to see you in trouble again."

Jake turned to Tuva, pushing Mina toward her. "Take her and get back to town quickly and stay there. I don't want either of you anywhere near Thorpe Prescott. Go to the store and stay there, but have Mina's father send the sheriff out here. Go now!"

Mina was openly crying as Jake put a hand on her shoulder. "I'll explain later, Mina. Right now, you're in danger. Please do as I ask."

Tuva pulled Mina away with her as Jake ran back to the barn. She helped the sobbing girl into the buggy and then climbed up on the seat beside her. Before she started Duncan, she turned to Mina.

"There's something very wrong about all this. I don't know what it is, but we're going to do what

Jake says." She turned the buggy and started down the road then exclaimed, "Oh no!"

"What?" Mina's head came up and she wiped at the tears on her face.

Tuva pointed. A man on horseback was almost upon them. Mina grabbed Tuva's arm.

"That's the man from town who's looking for Thorpe!"

sixteen

As Jake raced back to the barn he questioned if he made the right decision sending the girls back to town. There was a danger that they could meet up with Thorpe and his men between here and there, yet he couldn't allow them to stay here where they would certainly be in harm's way.

He was truly puzzled by Mina's declaration that he was her brother. It was nothing short of shocking to learn that she was Thorpe Prescott's sister, which made this whole situation even more troubling. Thorpe was his sworn enemy now. He had been his slave master, his tormentor, and now apparently wants to be his executioner, according to the man Keane and Thane were now keeping prisoner in the barn.

It was Thane's suggestion that they first find out if it were true that Thorpe was in town that led them to take the man called Cal prisoner. Thane and Keane scouted the town the night before and it was Keane who recognized the man as one of the crew on the ship and a cohort of Thorpe's. A knock on the head in a dark alley got them their prisoner, but other than learning that Thorpe intended to kill the two men, they got nothing more out of the man. He was now trussed up and gagged while they waited and watched for the others to appear.

Seeing the two girls at the farm had frightened Jake more than learning that Thorpe was out to kill him. Knowing the kind of man Thorpe was, Jake had no illusions that he would spare the women should they get in his way, but now learning that Mina was Thorpe's sister put a new twist on things. Did Thorpe know?

The others were anxious to find out why the girls had come.

"Was that Tuva with Mina?" Keane's concern was evident to all. "What were they doing here?"

Jake didn't know how to answer other than to say, "They wanted to warn us about Thorpe."

"Have they seen him? Has he actually talked to them about us?" Keane took a step closer to Jake and lowered his voice. "We can't let him get near them."

"I know." Jake looked over at Cal who was watching them with interest. There was an impression of evil about the man that stirred memories in Jake from his time on the ship. He felt Keane shudder as though he, too, were recalling those dark days. "No, we can't let him near them." Jake started for the door.

"Now, hold on a minute." Thane put out his hand. "We agreed to wait it out here until this feller made the first move. You can't risk being out in the open right now, son. Besides, we got some insurance with this one." He tapped the muzzle of his shotgun on Cal's head.

Jake knew the wisdom of the older man's words, but he still felt dread come over him. Something wasn't right, and he knew better than to underestimate Thorpe. He looked at Cal. "Thor would sacrifice him in a heartbeat if it meant he could get to me or Keane."

The prisoner's eyes widened at what Jake said then his eyebrows dropped into a scowl. Jake saw that he believed his words.

Keane leaned over to Jake and spoke only for his ears. "I wish Ma had gone to town too. I don't like that she's hiding out in the root cellar. They might find her there."

Thane overheard the words. "If they do, they'll get a dose of buckshot for their trouble. Don't worry about your Ma, boy. Right now we have to be ready ourselves. I'll be in the hayloft. You two better get in position."

Before Thane could move to the ladder leading to the loft above, a voice spoke from behind him. "You should have been in position already, boys."

Jake swung his rifle to aim at the voice and found he was pointing it directly at Mina. She was held in front of Thorpe, his hand over her mouth and his pistol pressing into her temple. Two other men came in with rifles in their hands and pistols at their sides. One had Tuva by the arm. She was tied and gagged and as the man stepped to one side of Thorpe, he shoved her into a hay pile in the corner. Keane stepped forward, but Jake held him back.

"We meet again, Preacher." He turned to Keane. "Did you miss me, Wheatly? I've missed both of you. Now, you're not going to try anything foolish, are you? It would be a shame to have to hurt this beautiful young girl, wouldn't it?"

All the men stood in tense silence, their guns held at the ready.

"You're going to put your weapons down now. Oh, don't worry. I won't kill this charming lady, but unless you obey right *now*, she will suffer from a bullet wound somewhere."

Jake gave a slight nod to the others and they slowly set down their guns. A more helpless feeling he had never had. Even on the ship when he could do nothing but take abuse from this man did he feel this powerless. He kept his eyes on Mina and tried not to let her see his fear for her.

It was Keane who spoke first. "You've come for *us*, Thorpe. Let the girls go."

At Keane's words Mina gave a jerk and twisted her head free of the hand over her mouth. "Thorpe? *You're* Thorpe?" She stared into Thorpe's eyes, but he twisted her arm behind her back until she cried out in pain.

"So, they've been telling you stories about me, have they? You mustn't believe everything you hear, my dear. I'm really not so bad once you get to know me."

"Boss."

One of Thorpe's men nodded in the direction of Cal who was trying to gain their attention. Thorpe turned to the captured man. "So, that's where you went. You ought to have known better than to let that happen." Without any warning, he raised the pistol and shot the man in the chest. Mina screamed.

"Now, what was I saying? Oh yes. Did you miss me, gentlemen? You see, I missed you. I was reminded every day of you when I was in the hospital and they were scraping burned skin off my arm. I've been reminded every day when I feel the tightness of the skin on my side and ribs. Burned because of you, I might point out. You were responsible for that fire. You dared to escape. Now you'll pay."

Jake only half-listened as he kept his eyes on Mina. She was in shock understandably, but he didn't think it had fully registered to her that the man holding onto her was her brother. All the while Thorpe ranted on, Jake was looking for a way to get Mina free of him. Thorpe's next order made Jake's mouth go dry.

"Tie her to that beam." He pulled out his whip. "No harm will come to your little friend if you cooperate. You give me any trouble and she'll feel its tongue."

Mina seemed dazed as one of the men tied her hands around the beam in the center of the barn.

"You going to whip your own *sister*, Thorpe?"

Only a twitch of the man's eyes indicated that he heard Jake. "Nice try, Preacher. My family is in Ohio."

Mina twisted her head around to see Thorpe. "You *are* Thorpe! No, please no!"

Thorpe walked to her and grabbed her face in his hand. "What's your name?"

Mina pulled away from him. "Wilhelmina Prescott. Let me go this instant!"

Thorpe laughed. "Very convincing. I don't care who you are. If these men do anything to displease me, you'll be the one to suffer for it. Have I made myself clear?"

"You are despicable!"

"Yes. I am." Thorpe motioned to his man. "Tie them, but be careful. I expect they'll try something." He slapped the whip in his hand. "I almost hope you do try something," he spoke directly to Jake.

The men cooperated. Jake worried about Keane. His anger was palpable and he was afraid Keane would try to rush the man who approached with a rope, but all Keane did was say, "Sorry, Pa. I'm so sorry."

"Did you speak, Wheatly? Did I give you permission to speak?" Thorpe's rage at this infraction made him raise the whip and snap it against Mina's back. She cried out in pain and Jake saw blood seep through the back of her torn shirtwaist. He held himself back but he couldn't keep the contempt from showing on his face as he turned to Thorpe.

"Did you want to say something, Preacher? Were you going to tell me that God loves me or something paltry like that, and that I shouldn't be such a bad boy?" Thorpe threw his head back and laughed then he grew serious. "I promised myself that death wasn't good enough for you two. Oh, don't misunderstand me, you'll die, but first you'll suffer.

Let's say we start with Wheatly. Get a rope up over that crossbeam. Wheatly, you'll have the honor of hanging your—what did you call him?—your *Pa*."

Keane's rage was so strong that Jake could see him trembling.

"No!"

Thorpe jerked his head toward Keane. "Did you speak?" He raised the whip, but Thane put up a hand.

"No need for that. Just do as the man says, son." He turned his back on Thorpe to face Keane, shifting his eyes from Jake's face to something behind him. Jake tried to recall what was behind them without turning his head or giving any indication that he had been given a signal from Thane.

The pitchfork.

Thorpe's anger was kindled again and he shouted, "I give the orders here!" There was another crack of his whip and a scream from Mina. As everyone's attention turned to her, Jake dove for the pitchfork. A rake was leaning next to it and he grabbed it and tossed it to Keane. Thane dropped to the ground as the Jake and Keane threw the farm implements as if they were javelins, one at the closest man with the rifle and the other directly at Thorpe.

In the back of Jake's mind was the third man who was to the right of Mina. He caught a quick glance of Tuva barreling into the man and knocking him off his feet. But he couldn't help either girl. Thorpe had fended off the pitchfork and had his whip raised to strike Jake. A shot rang out just as Jake tackled the man in front of him. He didn't know where the shot came from or who had been hit. He had all he could do to get untangled from the whip and keep Thorpe from getting to the pistol in his waistband.

But Thorpe wasn't struggling any longer. Jake grabbed the pistol and pointed it at him, but the man was breathing in deep gasps and no longer a threat. There was another shot, and Jake swung the pistol around to see the man who Tuva had knocked down was holding his chest. He dropped his rifle as he fell to the ground.

Three shadowy figures appeared in the back door of the barn. Jake couldn't make them out with the light behind them, but he saw that each carried a weapon. All three were pointing their guns at something beyond him. He kept his hand on Thorpe as he turned to see Keane and Thorpe's man wrestling and punching each other.

"Step away from him, Keane, so I can shoot him!" A man's voice shouted.

Keane turned at the sound of the voice, his face registering shock. "Mr. Rogers?" Just then Thorpe's man reached in his boot for a knife and was about to throw it when a shotgun blasted. The man screamed and fell to the ground, the knife flying out of his hand.

Thane grabbed the knife and got to his feet. He barely had time to right himself before Helma ran to him and threw herself into his arms, sobbing against him.

"There, there, my girl. I always said you were the best shot in the family." He turned his wife's face up toward him. "But you didn't stay put like you were supposed to."

Helma sniffed and reached for Keane and held him close. "I heard a woman scream. Then these people came and..."

Jake could still feel Thorpe's heartbeat under his hand. So much had happened in the past few seconds that he was having trouble comprehending it all, but right now he had to get to Mina.

"Watch him, will you, please, Mrs. Rogers?" He indicated Thorpe.

How the Rogers got there would have to be explained later. This couple had saved them once right after their escape from the sea, and now here they were again just when they were needed the most. A prayer of thankfulness was in Jake's heart though the words could not form in his brain. He held out his hand to get the knife from Thane before he knelt beside Mina who was on her knees, sobbing.

Gently and quickly Jake cut the ropes that bound her to the post. He turned her toward him and carefully put his arms around her, avoiding the welts that were forming on her back. Keane reached for the knife and went to attend to Tuva as Jake nestled Mina against him.

"Is he dead?" The voice was barely a whisper.

Jake looked over her head at Thorpe. His chest still rose and fell and he could hear the man's gasps for air. "No, but soon."

Mina pulled back and looked up at Jake. "We have to help him."

Her words stunned him. He looked at Mrs. Rogers who had been examining Thorpe's wound. She shook her head. As carefully as possible Jake said, "He's not going to make it, no matter what we do."

Mina laid her forehead against Jake's chest. Her voice was muffled when she spoke again. "We have to tell him how to go to heaven."

Every person in the barn was silent at her words. The only sounds were Thorpe's gasps for the air that was keeping him alive.

Jake met Keane's eyes and knew what he was thinking. They hated this man with all that was in them. He deserved to die. He deserved to go the hell.

The moment that thought came to him, Jake's mind was filled with verses he knew: *"Love your enemies; Do good to them that hate you; Be not overcome of evil, but overcome evil with good; pray for them that despitefully use you and persecute you."*

There were so many that kept flooding his mind, but the words *"...and such were some of you"* hit him the hardest. He was no better than Thorpe. He wanted to believe he was, but God's Word made it clear that *"all have sinned and come short of the glory of God. There is none righteous, no, not one."* He hadn't deserved God's grace any more than Thorpe did, yet God still offered it.

"Lord Jesus, help me." Jake pulled Mina to her feet beside him and led her to kneel before her dying brother. Jake took a deep breath.

"Thorpe, can you hear me?"

"I…hear…Preacher. Finish…me."

Mina took Thorpe's hand. "Thorpe, this is Wilhelmina, your sister. Please listen to what Jake has to say. It's very important."

Thorpe's eyelids fluttered but couldn't open. "Willie? It really...is...you?"

"Yes, Thorpe." Mina's tears dropped onto the hand she was holding. She turned beseechingly to Jake.

"Thorpe, I'm going to give it to you straight. You're not going to make it."

What must have meant to be a laugh came out as coughing and gasping for air from the wounded man. "That...will make...you...happy."

"I don't deny that, but I have no wish to see anyone go to hell. Thorpe, you can enter heaven's gates today. The Lord Jesus Christ took all the evil and sin you have in you and shed his holy blood for it on the cross. He was buried and he rose again. Your sins are forgiven by his sacrifice for you, Thorpe. All you do is believe that and heaven is yours today."

Thorpe's eyelids again fluttered and opened slightly. He stared into Jake's eyes then gave a slight, negative shake of his head. "Too...late...for...me. God...won't...take...me."

Jake became more insistent. "Listen. If I had time, I could quote you verse after verse about how *all* sin has been taken care of by Jesus. You know you're a sinner, Thorpe, and you know you could never be good enough for heaven, but what you seem to think is that Jesus's blood wasn't good enough for you. In Colossians it says, '...having forgiven you all trespasses.' And 'In whom we have redemption through his blood, even the forgiveness of sins.'

"You're the most evil man I've ever met, Thorpe, but I'm no better in God's eyes because he says that 'all have sinned.' We're all in the same boat.

But God offers forgiveness of those sins through the cross if you'll only believe it."

"Please believe, Thorpe. I want you in heaven. I want to see my brother again." Mina pleaded.

Thorpe opened his eyes to look at Mina. "I...hurt...you."

"And I forgive you. You've hurt the Lord too, and he wants to forgive you. Just believe him, Thorpe."

"I...don't...deserve..."

"None of us do," Jake spoke up. "It's called grace."

"If...He'll...take a...sinner...like me..." Thorpe coughed. "Thank...you...Jesus."

He went limp.

Mina looked anxiously at Mrs. Rogers who bent over Thorpe. She shook her head.

"He's gone."

Mina got to her feet and walked into Jake's embrace. "He's with the Lord now. Thank you, Jake, for—"

"NO!"

They all turned to Keane who had shouted the word. Without a backward look at any of them, Keane raced from the barn.

Keane ran until his heart was pounding and he could no longer catch his breath. Then he walked. He wanted to get as far away from the scene in the barn as he could.

All the while that Jake and Mina were talking to Thorpe, Keane felt bitterness grow in him. He didn't want Thorpe to get saved! He didn't want his tormentor to enjoy the glory of heaven! The man was a murderer! They all saw him shoot Cal in cold blood. He and Jake had seen him drown Tommy Rogers and others. He had whipped, tormented, and persecuted so many.

Keane relived the moment when Thorpe commanded him to hang his father. He saw again in his mind how he whipped Mina. He heard his evil laugh over and over until he put his hands over his ears to block it out.

No. If God was going to save Thorpe Prescott, then Keane wanted nothing to do with God.

Keane put his hands on his hips and looked around him. He was near the tree where Tuva sang. Again Keane felt a shudder run through him as he recalled watching Tuva, tied and gagged, get to her feet and ram into Thorpe's man to knock him down. The bravery of the girl amazed him, and he knew that without that action, things could have gone so much worse for those in the barn.

He had cut Tuva's ropes loose and held her as tightly as she held onto him. They cared for each other. Perhaps he was in love with her. He knew he was more afraid for her during that ordeal than he was for himself. But as Jake continued to talk to Thorpe, Keane had started to back away from Tuva. He recalled her puzzled look as he put space between himself and the others, not wanting to be a part of helping Thorpe see his salvation.

"What do I do now?" He said the words out loud. It wasn't a prayer. He was done with that.

It occurred to him that if he stayed on the farm, he would constantly be challenged either by Jake or his parents in his belief, and he couldn't endure that. He loved his family and he owed Jake a debt that he could never repay, but he knew he wouldn't be able to face them day after day. Not now.

He started walking again, this time toward town. He'd stop at the bank and get a little money and then head to the northern part of the state. There were logging camps he could work in and he'd heard of mining camps starting up that needed men. His conscience pricked him at how his folks would feel about him leaving again, but it had to be done. Besides, Jake would be there to help them now. He'd write and let them know where he was.

And there was Tuva. Keane's step faltered and he looked back at the tree, seeing and hearing her voice in his mind. He shook his head. It wouldn't work. Tuva loved God with all her heart. It was evident in her songs and her life. She could never live with someone like him who no longer believed.

Keane picked up his pace. The sooner he was away, the better for all.

seventeen

Tuva was startled when Keane shouted "NO!" and ran from the barn. She started after him but was held back by Helma who took her arm.

"Let him go, dear. Give him a few moments."

Tuva nodded and returned the older woman's embrace, but she was worried. She didn't know Keane very well yet, but she had seen his face, and she didn't think a few moments were going to change his reaction to what had just happened.

She watched Jake and Mina stand together and hold onto each other for comfort and support. There was no hiding the feelings they had for one another, and she was glad for her friend. She thought of the embrace she and Keane had shared and knew that even though there was much she still did not know about him, she loved him. Her fear for him had been so great that she had given no thought to her own safety when she ran headlong into the man with the rifle. She only wished she could have done more.

Helma was taking Mina from Jake now to tend to her wounds, so Tuva came alongside and took Mina's other arm. Mina turned to her and threw herself into Tuva's embrace.

"Oh, Tuva! I'm so sorry I got you involved in this! You didn't want to come and I made you and look what happened!" Mina burst into tears again.

"Shh. It's all right now. Let's get you to the house and get cleaned up. It's over now."

The other woman, the one they called Mrs. Rogers, spoke up. "May I come along with you ladies?"

"Certainly," Helma motioned for her to follow. "You are the ones who really saved the day here. I thank the Lord you showed up when you did."

"I'm just glad you didn't decide to use that shotgun on us!" The woman's laugh seemed to bring the situation back to normal to Tuva. She looked curiously at her, and Mrs. Rogers smiled in return.

"Let's get the young lady comfortable and I'll explain my presence," she said.

They were on their way to the house when they saw a wagon and a person on horseback approaching.

"Goodness! What now?" Helma exclaimed.

"It's Mother and Father!" Mina pointed. "But who's the man?"

Tuva shielded her eyes with her hand. "That would be the sheriff, and look over there." Tuva pointed to a group of men who were standing near the chicken coop.

"Why, those are our Indian friends!" Helma exclaimed.

The sheriff jumped from his horse and ran up to the women. "The Indians came to town with the news that there was trouble out here. What's going on?"

Thane came from the barn and quickly got the attention of the newcomers, giving them a short version of what had occurred. The sheriff hurried to the barn, and Thane went to thank the Indians for their help. Mr. Prescott helped his wife down and she hurried to catch up to the women.

"Mina! What has happened to you? Are you all right? Is Thorpe really here?"

Tuva stood back as Mina quickly told her mother and father the basics of what had happened. When the couple learned that their son was dead, there was stunned silence. As Mina went on to tell of Thorpe's acceptance of Christ. Mr. Prescott held his weeping wife and said, "Praise God for that."

He left them to continue on to the house while he joined the others in the barn.

As Helma heated water to wash Mina's wounds, the rest of the story came out in bits and pieces. After Mina and Tuva told about what had gone on in the barn, Helma took up the tale.

"I was in the root cellar where Thane made me promise to stay." She pointed to the trap door in the floor of the kitchen. "But then I heard a woman scream. That must have been you, dear." She patted Mina's arm. "I knew more was going on than we had counted on, so I decided to see if I could help. That's when I came upon these people sneaking up to the house."

Mrs. Rogers nodded. "I should explain who we are. When Jake and Keane escaped from the ship in that storm, they found our cabin and came to us for help. We learned from them about Tommy, our son, and how he died." She paused and looked directly at Mina and her mother. "I know now that he was your son and your brother, and I'm sorry for your loss, but you have to understand that at the time we had nothing but hatred for the man who murdered our son."

Mina nodded and Mrs. Prescott wiped at tears that were falling.

"Well, this man—Thorpe—came looking for information about Jake and Keane. I don't remember what story he told us about who he was, but we saw through it and knew he was up to no good. We checked further in town and found out he was from their ship, and he was the one who…who drowned Tommy."

At her words, the women gasped in unison. Mrs. Prescott put her hand on Mrs. Rogers' arm, her voice coming out as a sob. "I am so sorry."

Mrs. Rogers nodded and cleared her throat. "We found out that Thorpe and some men took a train east, and it bothered us. The mister and I talked about it and decided that we better get a warning to Jake and Keane, so we took it on ourselves to play detective and follow them. It wasn't hard. Most people remembered them and were willing to help us. Anyway, we found them here and learned that this was Keane's home and knew there was going to be trouble. We were 'sneaking' as Mrs. Wheatly said, trying to figure out if they were in the house or the barn."

Helma spoke up. "So I aimed my shotgun at them and demanded to know who they were and what they were up to. I got enough of a gist of what they were saying to figure they were on our side when we heard a woman—that was you, Mina—scream again. We hightailed it to the barn and the rest you know."

Mina winced as Helma dabbed at her cuts. "But, Mother, the good news is that Thorpe accepted Jesus before he died. We'll see him again and all the evil will be gone forever."

Mrs. Prescott cried openly at her daughter's words. The others offered comfort, and there was an awkward silence until Helma suggested they prepare a meal. That gave them all something to do and helped the atmosphere return to some semblance of normalcy.

"I'd like to see him."

Mrs. Prescott's words caused them to stop their labors. The women looked at each other until Tuva spoke up.

"I'll take you, Mrs. Prescott."

Mina thanked Tuva with a grateful look. Tuva could only imagine that it would be difficult for her friend to go back to the scene in the barn.

Tuva led Mrs. Prescott to the barn and called to Jake to take her in. Tuva had no wish to go back in herself so she leaned on the side of the building and looked out over the fields, wondering where Keane was and when he would return. Her knees felt weak now that she had time to reflect on what had happened. She had never been that close to death before, and she had never witnessed another human being dying. She didn't realize she was trembling until Thane stood beside her and took her arm.

"Here now. You need to sit down, Tuva."

She allowed him to help her to the ground, and he sat beside her. "How is Mina?" he asked.

"Helma's getting her cleaned up and bandaged, and they're fixing something to eat."

Thane chuckled, startling Tuva. "Leave it to Helma to think of food."

Tuva smiled.

"You're worried about Keane, aren't you?"

"Yes."

Thane stretched out his legs. "He's going to have to deal with this like we all are. I can't imagine it would be easy to forgive someone like that Thorpe, but if God can do it, we should follow his example." He grinned at Tuva. "I know I'm preaching to the wrong person, but if you should happen to have a talk with my son, you might want to relay that to him." He tilted his head to one side as he studied Tuva. "You sweet on my son?"

Tuva felt a blush creep up her face.

"Ah, that seems to say it all. I hope he realizes what a treasure you are." Thane started to get to his feet, his movements awkward and obviously painful. "Well, come on. Let's get everyone something to eat and then I'll take you home. I think you need your folks about now, don't you?"

Tuva nodded. "But I can walk—"

"No, none of that. I won't rest until I see you're home safely."

"And Keane?"

Thane looked out over the fields as if searching for him. "God will take care of Keane."

Mina sat between her parents as they rode home in the dark. The buggy seat was a bit crowded, but no one seemed to mind. Mina felt secure with both her father and mother's arms around her.

It was decided that the sheriff would take the bodies of the men back to town in the wagon the Prescotts had rented to follow their daughter. When Mina asked her parents how they knew to come to the Wheatlys, they told her about their strange interaction with Mr. and Mrs. Rogers.

"They came into the store, and Mr. Rogers asked if we were the Prescotts and if Thorpe was with us. We were naturally cautious in our reply, and I think that made them suspicious of us. They wanted to know where the Wheatly farm was and they left." Mina's father re-counted the story. "Then the sheriff came in and said that the Rogers had been there and told some story about our son planning to kill Keane Wheatly and Jake Rodwell and wanted to know if we knew anything about it. After that, about four or five Indian men came in the store looking for the sheriff and said there was trouble at the Wheatlys. Seems they had seen Thorpe and his men following you girls. That's when we knew we had to get out here in a hurry."

"And we didn't know for sure where you were," Mrs. Prescott added. "We just knew that if

Thorpe was around, there was going to be trouble." Her voice broke. "I had no idea how much trouble he has caused."

"But we're going to try to forget that now, Mother."

Mina saw her mother smile in the darkness. "How is it possible to be sad and happy at the same time?"

Mr. Prescott cleared his throat. "There was a telegram in Thorpe's pocket."

"A telegram?" Mina turned to her father.

"It wasn't opened, and it had someone else's name on it, but when I read it, I saw that it was a copy of the telegram we sent him in Seattle. It was the one telling him that we were here in Ulen instead of in Ohio. He really didn't know we were here."

"Do you think if he had known it would have made a difference?"

"I'd like to think so."

It was difficult for Mina to go to sleep that night. Understandably, her painful back was part of the trouble, but more so was the continual replaying of the events of the day that wouldn't give her peace. She tried to give her thoughts over to the Lord, but she couldn't stop seeing the horrors the day produced.

Mina threw aside the quilt as she got up and went to the window. Keane hadn't returned. That was a new worry for the Wheatlys, and they had already had to endure his absence once before. Tuva seemed to stand up to everything in her normal, steady way, but Mina had seen Thane gently help her into the wagon to take her home. He was concerned about her, and so was Mina.

The Rogers were a conundrum. The couple were dear to Jake and Keane because of their help to them after the night they escaped from the ship, but it was the Rogers' bullet that killed Thorpe, and even though it had been necessary, it was still something that could cause a barrier between them and the Prescotts, not that Mina wished it to be.

But how can it be helped? Mina's thoughts troubled her as she looked out at the starry night. Mrs. Rogers admitted that they did not wish to return to their home in Washington, but did that mean that they would settle here? Could they form a friendship with Thorpe's death and the death of their son Tommy between them?

Helma had been a rock through the whole ordeal, but when Thane returned from taking Tuva home, Mina saw her go to her husband and question him with her eyes. When he shook his head, her tears had come unbidden. She was worried about her son.

Mina rubbed her forehead. So many people affected by the evil of her brother, and yet, she had to rejoice that he came to the Lord before he died.

"Mina?"

Her father's voice made Mina start.

"It's just me. Can't sleep?" He came to stand beside her.

Mina leaned against her father's arm. "I just keep thinking of all the people who had to suffer and still suffer because of Thorpe. I mean, I'm glad he's with the Lord now, but I grieve for those he's hurt."

Her father was silent a moment. "You know how we always hear people say that it takes time to get over things? I guess we're finding that out now. It's going to take time before the wounds on your back heal, just as it's going to take time for our hearts to heal. But, Mina." He turned her toward him. "We have God as our comfort. He'll see us through."

Mina smiled up at him.

"Okay, back to bed now, sweetheart. You need to rest."

Mina moved to the bed and climbed in. "You like Jake, don't you, Father?"

Mr. Prescott stopped in the doorway. "He's a fine man, but he has wounds that are still healing too. Give him time. You both need to move past this before you know what the future holds for you."

Mina positioned herself on her side, avoiding the painful welts on her back. "But you do like him, right?"

Her father laughed softly. "Yes, I like him, and I dare say, we'll be seeing a lot more of him. Now go to sleep."

Mina smiled into her pillow and let sleep overtake her.

The next morning Mina woke stiff and sore. Her mother helped her dress and forbade her to do anything but rest. Mina wanted to argue but found the advice to be just what she needed. After her sleepless night, she was able to nap, and the quiet of the day gave her time for reading her Bible and praying. By afternoon she was feeling more like her old self and she descended the stairs to the store.

"Where's Father?"

"Wilhelmina! What are you doing up?" her mother scolded. She took Mina's hands. "Your father went to take care of arrangements."

"You mean for a funeral?"

Mrs. Prescott nodded, and Mina noticed the dark circles under her eyes. "Yes, for Thorpe. The sheriff will see to the others. We don't know if anyone will come for them, but something should be done. The sheriff sent wires to Seattle to see if there are any family members who should be notified."

Mina nodded. "Can I help you?" She pointed to the storeroom.

"You really should be resting, but if you're up to it, then maybe it would be good to keep you busy for a while."

They worked together in silence. When her mother was called to wait on a customer, Mina continued to fill the shelves with supplies. Life went on. It seemed strange to be doing something so ordinary after their terrible experience, but it was also comforting, as if by doing so she was saying that things were going to be okay. Mina turned her head when a familiar voice caught her ear. She stood so quickly she upset the cask of herring, spilling the brine onto the floor and over her skirt. She swept through the curtained doorway and met Jake as he stepped toward her.

"Wilhelmina!" Mrs. Prescott wrinkled her nose. "What have you done now?"

Mina looked down at her wet skirt. The aroma of pickled fish filled the air. She looked up into Jake's eyes and saw he couldn't contain a grin.

"Mud, pickles, and now fish! I have got to buy you some perfume."

She couldn't help it. She laughed. Then Jake laughed. And finally, Mrs. Prescott threw up her hands and joined them. Mr. Prescott came through the back door of the store and eyed them cautiously, which made them laugh even more. He broke into a grin when he saw the mess his daughter had created.

"Better go get cleaned up, Mina. I'll take care of this."

Mina looked at Jake. "You'll wait?"

"Yes, but hurry. I need to take the train."

Concern stopped Mina. "You're leaving?"

"Only for a short time. Hurry, and I'll explain."

Mina's mother followed her up the stairs to assist her in changing. "At least you only got your skirt soiled this time," she teased her daughter. She saw Mina's anxious expression. "Now, don't start worrying. Jake must have a good reason. Go on now."

Jake led Mina to the bench outside the store where they could converse somewhat privately. She watched him, wanting to ask questions, but exercised patience to give him time to tell her what he was doing.

Jake motioned to her back. "Still hurts, I bet."

"I'm okay."

"Could you sleep?"

"Not well." She couldn't wait any longer. "Why do you have to take the train, Jake?"

He sighed. "I'm going to go after Keane."

Her eyes widened. "He left on the train last night? Where did he go? How do you know?"

"He left a note. He got the bank manager to go to the bank and open it and he took out some money. He left the note with him. I checked the station master at the train, and he said Keane got on last night and headed north."

"What did the note say?"

Jake hesitated. "He said he needs to get away and think. He's going to work in the lumber camps if he can."

Mina wondered if the note said more than that, but Jake didn't elaborate. "It's because Thorpe accepted Christ. Keane wanted him to go to hell." The words were blunt.

"Mina, you have to understand—"

"Oh, I understand. If he were anyone but my brother, I would probably feel the same way." She stopped abruptly and stared at the ground as if she could find an answer there. "I'm so sorry, Jake."

"You have nothing to be sorry about." Jake took her hand and turned her toward him. "I'm sorry we brought all this trouble to your doorstep, as it were."

"But he was my brother! How could you ever love someone who was related to him? Oh!" Mina clapped her free hand over her mouth when she realized what she'd said. "I shouldn't have said—"

"I'm glad you did." Jake studied her features until she was blushing. "You are a very easy person to love, Mina Prescott." He cleared his throat and looked from side to side, indicating that this was not the place for a declaration of love. "I'd like to tell you more about that when I get back. May I call on you then?"

Mina nodded while she slowly took her hand away, revealing her smile. They rose to their feet with Jake still holding her hand.

"Until then. You take care of yourself."

"Please be careful, Jake. I'll be praying for you and for Keane. And hurry back."

eighteen

Working in the woods was an entirely new experience for Keane. It took him very little time to find a camp willing to take him on, and he was finding the work exhausting and exhilarating at the same time. The days were getting colder and the ground was freezing even though the first snow had yet to fall.

They weren't felling trees yet. In fact, most of the men who would be at the camp still needed to arrive, but there was time. Keane was given the job of helping build a cook shack in the new location the owner had chosen. He had never done much of that type of work and found that he enjoyed it. He also liked the tall trees that surrounded the camp and the view of the river beyond. When he first arrived only a couple of weeks ago, he had felt claustrophobic. All his life he had vistas of open fields around him. Even when he was shanghaied he had the open water for scenery. Never had his vision been so limited, yet there was a beauty about it that captivated him.

"When you're finished with lunch, Wheatly, they could use your help in the barn."

"Yes, sir." Keane nodded to the whiskered foreman. He was a good boss and easy to work for, at least he was after he made it clear to Keane that his attitude would have to change if he was going to stay on with the crew. Keane recalled the day he arrived.

"We can't have any hotheads around here, Wheatly. The work is dangerous enough without having to watch our backs too. You got a beef with someone, you take care of it now or find a new place to work."

"I have no problem with anyone."

"Good. I can use you."

Keane made his way to the barns and started brushing down the horses. This was his favorite job and reminded him of home. He paused. He didn't want to think of home and what his parents were doing. He shook himself free of his thoughts, but when the other worker in the barn began whistling, Keane recognized the tune as one of the hymns Tuva sang. He clenched his jaw.

"Do you have to whistle?" he barked at the man.

The whistling stopped, and the man poked his head around the corner. Seeing Keane, he grinned and started whistling again. Keane grabbed the brush in his hand and flung it at the man, narrowly missing him. The brush crashed against a post. The man grinned again and went back to whistling.

"Seems you have a temper."

Keane swung around to the doorway. "What are you doing here?"

Jake stood with his arms folded in front of him. "You know why I'm here."

"I'm not going back. I want nothing to do with any of them."

"So you're going to punish them by staying away?"

Keane was aware that the whistling had stopped, and the man was listening to them. He moved to the doorway and brushed past Jake, knowing he would follow him. When they had gone some distance and had privacy, Keane spoke again.

"You're wasting your time. I'm done with God, I'm done with people who coddle a murderer, and I'm done with you!"

"And your folks? They lost you once and it almost killed them. Why are you doing this to them?"

Keane didn't answer. He stood facing Jake with his hands on his hips, but his head was turned away and he stared off into the distance.

"If it's me, I'll leave. I don't want to stand between you and your folks, but I think it's much deeper. You—"

"Don't start preaching at me! I don't want to hear it!" Keane held out an arm to ward Jake away from him. "If you all want to be with Thorpe in heaven, you just go right ahead. I don't want to go anywhere he's going to be. You hear me? I'm done with it all. If God takes a murderer like that to heaven, then I don't want to go there! Now get out of here!"

Keane started to walk away, but Jake spoke after him. "Okay, I'll go. But you can't get away from God, Keane. No matter if you're faithful to him or not, he promised to be faithful to you. And it's a good thing too because we don't deserve heaven. None of us! Only by his grace, *only by his grace*, Keane!" Jake repeated the words louder as Keane moved away from him.

"Anything I can do?"

The man who had been whistling in the barn came and stood beside Jake. Together they watched Keane walk away and then break into a run. "Looks like he can't get away from you fast enough."

Jake sighed. He had wanted so much to reach Keane and bring him home with him, but he could see it was not going to happen. He turned to the man and held out his hand. "Jake Rodwell."

The man shook his hand. "Name's Thomas. Heard what you was sayin' to him. He's runnin' from God, huh?"

Jake nodded.

"Been my experience that the only thing you can do is let him run until he's run out. I'll keep an eye on him. Hopefully he'll get some sense knocked back into his head before too long."

Jake turned to look at the man. Thomas wasn't very tall and was thin and wiry with a short, gray striped beard. "Thanks, Thomas. Would you do something for me? Would you write and let me know how he's doing? His folks will worry."

"Sure. Not much good at spellin', but I'll try. Gotta warn ya though. Mail goes through only once a month when the snow starts up."

"That's okay. Any news will help. And, Thomas, pray for him." Jake left an address and some money for writing materials.

Jake fought his discouragement as he got off the train in Ulen. He wished he had better news to report to the Wheatlys about Keane, but he would have to be honest. About his own future, he was uncertain. He would stay on with the Wheatlys and help with the work until Keane returned, but after that, he wasn't sure what to do.

His thoughts turned to Mina. Whatever he did, Mina would be a part of it. He was sure of that now. The sting of losing Eva and their child had passed. He would always love Eva and the memory of her, but he knew there was a life for him with Mina and that he loved her dearly. Seeing her in danger hadn't been necessary for him to realize that. He knew.

His steps took him to the General Store. He smiled at the name above the door. No matter what Mina's last name was now—Austinson, Asleson, or Prescott—soon he hoped to make it Rodwell. The bell jangled as he pushed the door open. He looked eagerly for sight of Mina either behind the counter or in the storeroom, but there was a man behind the counter, a man Jake had never seen before. He stepped forward, looking about him as he did.

"Afternoon. What can I do for you?"

"Uh, hello. I'm looking for the Prescotts."

"Oh. They've been gone for about a week or so now, I guess. Sure did appreciate them handling the store while my partner and I were away. Name's Ole Asleson." The man held out his hand.

Jake was stunned. He took the man's hand and shook it and stated his name. "They're gone, you say? A week? Where did the Prescotts go?"

"Rodwell? Say, I have a letter for you. Let me see here." The man searched through some papers on the counter behind him while Jake stared at him with a sinking feeling. If Mina left a letter that meant she wasn't in town.

"Yes, here it is. Those Prescotts are mighty fine people. Took real good care of things here. Only thing is, the storeroom kind of smells like fish." Mr. Asleson mumbled something else, but Jake didn't catch it. He thanked the man for the letter and exited the store. Finding a seat outside, he sat down, took a deep breath, and ripped open the envelope.

He was on his feet in an instant after reading the one line letter. All it said was: *Jake, don't leave town. We're at the City Hotel. Love, Mina.*

He found himself running down the middle of the street to get to the hotel, not caring that people were staring at him. He pushed open the door of the hotel and came face-to-face with Mr. Prescott. Even in his haste to see Mina, Jake noted that the hair on the man's temples had grayed since he was gone.

"Jake! I'm glad to see you found us. How did it go looking for young Wheatly?"

Jake gripped the man's hand. "Not good, I'm afraid. Is Mina here? You're not working at the store any longer? You said Mina was here?"

Mr. Prescott laughed. "Mina and her mother are upstairs. We haven't made it definite yet, but we're thinking of purchasing the hotel and running it. The economy in the country is not going well, and we certainly don't want to return to the city."

Jake let out the breath he had been holding. "So you're not leaving town. Good!"

"No. We did struggle with the decision of whether to stay or leave, you know, with the bad feelings about our son and all, but the Wheatlys came and talked to us and said that there was no reason we should feel we had to go. There is the issue with Keane's feelings. You say it didn't go well?"

Jake shook his head. "I found him and tried to talk to him, but I'm afraid he's not ready to listen to reason. I'm sorry."

Mr. Prescott nodded. "I am too. We certainly don't want to be a constant reminder to him—"

"It's not you folks. Keane has to deal with this between him and the Lord. I thought he had put it all behind him when we got here, but he hasn't let it go yet."

A motion on the stairway caught Jake's eye and he looked up to see Mina hurrying down the steps in a most unladylike fashion.

"Wilhelmina!" He heard Mrs. Prescott call after her daughter. "You're going to fall and break your neck!"

Mina didn't slow her steps as she raced across the entryway to Jake, her hands held out to him. He took them and smiled at her, aware that Mr. Prescott was grinning at them.

"May I steal Mina away for a few minutes, sir?"

"Of course. I think the sample room is empty at the moment." He pointed to a doorway.

Jake took Mina's arm and led her in. If he had hoped for privacy, he was disappointed as there was a large window looking onto the street. Nevertheless, once they stepped out of sight around the doorway, he pulled Mina into his embrace.

"I was so scared when the man at the store said you'd left." He released her but kept her hands in his as he smiled down at her.

"Oh, Jake!" Mina pulled free and tried to push her hair into a semblance of order. The loose bun was coming undone because of her race down the stairway, and dark wisps of hair framed her face in a most intriguing manner. She tugged at the apron strings around her waist. "I shouldn't have let you see me like this. Mother and I were cleaning upstairs, but when I heard your voice, I just couldn't wait to see you."

"You're lovely, even more beautiful than I remembered." He pulled her close once again. "I missed you."

A noise from the next room reminded him that they were not alone. He stepped back once again and led her to a chair. Mina's rosy cheeks and shining eyes were his undoing. He leaned closer and whispered, "I love you."

Tears sparkled in Mina's eyes as she smiled and nodded, seemingly unable to speak.

"I should wait for a more appropriate moment, but I never want to be apart from you again, Mina. Will you be my wife?"

"Jake! Yes, oh, yes!"

Jake started to reach for her but people happened to pass by the window just then, making him aware that he had chosen a rather public place to make his proposal. He didn't realize his frustration was evident until he heard Mina's quiet laugh.

"You must think me uncivilized not to do a better job of this, but how about if I come back this evening and take you to dinner?"

"You don't have to do anything like that, Jake. The answer is yes whether you ask me now or later. I fell in love with you when I heard you speak in church. I want nothing more than to be your wife."

Jake was elated. "I'll talk to your father and get permission. There is so much we have to discuss. May I return tomorrow?"

"And the day after that, and the one after that?" Mina teased.

Jake grinned. Then Mina became serious. "Tell me about Keane. Did you find him? Did he come back with you?"

They talked longer than Jake intended. He knew the Wheatlys were anxious to hear from him, so he reluctantly stood. "I admit I want to get married right away, Mina, but I have no home to offer you yet. I'm not even sure how I'm going to support you, although I have funds for some time yet. Fortunately, with all the banks struggling these days, I kept most of my money out of the bank. More than anything I want to please the Lord with our decisions. Our time on this earth is short, and we need to use it wisely."

Mina placed her hand on Jake's arm. "I don't want to wait long either, Jake, but whatever decisions we make, I'll be by your side."

It was hard to leave Mina, but Jake finally let her go. Once she had ascended the stairway, he turned to Mr. Prescott, who was eyeing him suspiciously.

Jake met the man's eyes.

"Nothing would make me happier, son." Mr. Prescott spoke without preamble.

"But I haven't asked you yet," Jake grinned.

"Okay, ask."

"Sir, may I have permission to marry your daughter?" Jake's tone was formal.

"Nothing would make me happier, son."

The men laughed and shook hands. Jake's heart was light as he began the walk back to the Wheatly farm. He praised God with a thankful heart then prayed for Keane. He didn't know what the future was going to bring, but he was ready to face the future.

nineteen

"The economy's really taking a beating." Thane remarked at the breakfast table. "I guess we should feel fortunate we don't have much to lose or we'd feel bad if we lost it." His joke made Jake smile.

"Hard for young folks to get started though," Helma put in. "Have you and Mina looked at the Zimmerman place yet?" she asked Jake.

"We have." Jake sopped up the syrup on his plate with a pancake. "Mina likes it, and I like that it's close by so I can still come give you folks a hand."

"Don't worry so much about us. Keane will be back before long and he'll run the place." Thane spoke matter-of-factly as he always did when referring to his son's return.

Helma exchanged glances with Jake. Thane's arthritis was bothering him more now that the winter months were staking a claim on the countryside. Jake offered her a smile that she returned, although a slight frown still etched her face.

"I do have some news." Jake straightened and held up his cup as Helma added hot coffee to it. "I've been asked to fill the pulpit temporarily and possibly permanently if the board determines I'm a good fit for the congregation."

"That's wonderful!" Helma exclaimed.

"I wonder, though, if I can handle both preaching and farming. The winter months should be okay, but it's those long summer days of planting and harvesting that have me concerned. I wouldn't wish to shortchange God's work."

"You can handle it, son, especially with Keane and I helping you out in the busy season. Don't forget you'll have a wife to give you a hand as well." Thane spoke with confidence.

Helma glanced at her husband again before turning to Jake. "How are the wedding plans coming along?"

"I hear things about fabric and lace, but I don't know what it all means," Jake admitted, his eyebrows raised comically. "We're still planning on spring. Mina's busy helping her parents get the hotel organized and…" He paused and shot Thane a quick look. "We're still hoping Keane will be here for it."

Thane pushed back his chair and stood. "You can count on it. Well, snow or no snow, the animals expect to be fed. We'd better get at it. Thank you, dear, for breakfast."

"Oh, wait a minute!" Helma pulled an envelope out of her pocket. "I forgot to tell you what the Rogers said in their letter."

Thane leaned on the back of his chair. "How do they like South Dakota so far?"

Helma scanned the letter. "They say that where they are is quite beautiful with the Black Hills out their window. They're settling in and trying to get used to the cold weather. I bet that was a surprise for them." Helma added then she continued reading. "They say they found a good church and that they are well and hope we are doing well also. They are happy about the news that Jake is getting married."

Helma folded the letter again. "I wish they would have stayed on here. I really liked them, but I understand that they felt it unwise to be a constant reminder to the Prescotts about their son."

Jake nodded but said nothing. The results of Thorpe's actions continued to affect the lives of the people around them. The last letter he received from Thomas at the logging camp revealed no change in Keane's attitude.

"What will it take, Lord, for Keane to see how sufficient your grace is?"

Keane had about had it with Thomas. He didn't know if Thomas had requested to be his partner or if the foreman had assigned him to Keane, but the man was everywhere Keane went. It wouldn't be so bad if he would only quit talking. It didn't matter that Keane ordered him not to talk to him about God, Thomas just kept on with his comments and his verses and his whistling.

Logging wasn't bad. Keane had become accustomed to the routine and relished the hard work. He didn't care much for the living conditions or the food, but it was a job and he was earning some wages. The thought that his parents could certainly use the money crossed his mind, but he quickly quelled it, leaving him with a guilty feeling that he tried to brush away. At night on his bunk the thoughts were not easily swept aside. As much as he tried not to think on it, he knew in his heart that he was causing his folks pain and that they didn't deserve that.

There were times his heart softened and he longed to go back. Just before sleep took him at night, he saw the images of home in his mind—his mother with her apron on, busy in the kitchen, his father with his gnarled hands around a coffee cup, his comfortable bed with the bright patchwork quilt on it, the open fields of waving grain, Tuva...Tuva, with her royal crown of braids. Then other nights he relived being shackled in the hold of the ship, being whipped into submission, fighting the storm with Jake in the tiny rowboat, seeing Tommy Rogers' lifeless body. Those times he reaffirmed his hatred for Thorpe Prescott and the reason he could no longer be among people who had forgiven him.

He was tormented either way. The good memories only made him long for the life he had turned his back on, and the bad memories fed his hatred.

Keane headed to the woods the next day. The air was crisp and the white snow blinding. He was eager to get to work, eager to have something to do to keep his mind from returning to thoughts of home. He arrived at the area the foreman had assigned to him and Thomas and prepared to take down the first tree. He didn't bother waiting for his nemesis to join him, but he heard Thomas running to catch up to him.

"Boss says you're wanted back at camp." Thomas was out of breath from running, and his beard was already crusted with ice crystals.

"Why?"

"Dunno. He says to tell you to hightail it back there on the double." Thomas took the saw from Keane's hand. "You want I should go with you?"

"No."

Keane turned to go back just as Thomas began whistling "When the Roll is Called Up Yonder". He cringed and tried to block out the sound but he couldn't help recalling that Thomas had told him the history of the new hymn whether he cared to hear it or not. The author was a Sunday school teacher and one of his pupils had missed attendance, so he visited the child's home and found that she needed a doctor for pneumonia. The man thought on what missing a roll call in heaven would be like and thus wrote the song.

Keane shook his head, trying to dispel Thomas and his confounded whistling from his head. He didn't want to think on such things. After he saw what the foreman wanted, he'd request a new partner. He didn't think he could endure another day with

Thomas. He spotted the foreman by the cook shack and hurried over to him.

"You wanted me, boss?"

The foreman looked at him and then looked past him. "Where's Thomas?"

"Back at the site. He told me you needed me?"

The foreman frowned, puzzling Keane by the man's reaction. "I told him—well, never mind, you're here. Go on in. The cook will explain." He walked away as if in a hurry to be gone from there.

Keane didn't know what to think. He'd never been given instructions from the cook before, but he might as well see what the man needed.

The room was dark to Keane after being in the bright sunlight. He squinted to make out the cook at the back of the building.

"You need something?" He called out. "Foreman sent me."

"This way." The cook motioned for him to follow him.

More curious than concerned, Keane walked to where the man held back a curtain. By now he could see more clearly, and he recognized the boy lying on the cot there. He was the cookee, the cook's helper.

He looked from the boy to the cook. The cook pointed to a stool beside the cot.

"What?"

The cook pointed again and gave Keane a prod toward the stool. "He wants to talk to you."

"To *me*?"

The cook dropped the curtain, leaving Keane alone with the boy. Keane took a closer look and saw the boy's face was flushed and that he was laboring to breathe. He stood in indecision just as the boy opened his eyes.

"You're not Thomas." The boy's voice was weak, but Keane heard him.

"You want Thomas? I'll go get him." Keane backed away, but the boy raised a hand to stop him.

"No. I...I can't wait. Come here."

Keane felt his heart start pounding. He didn't know why he was there, but he was afraid he wasn't going to like finding out.

The boy reached for Keane's sleeve and gave it a slight tug. Keane lowered himself to the stool and waited.

"They say I've got...pneumonia and that I might die." The boy coughed as he struggled to say the words.

Keane's first reaction was to run. *Thomas!* The word pneumonia instantly made him think of the song Thomas was whistling and the reason it was written. Thomas sent him here on purpose, but Keane was having none of it. He rose and pushed the curtain aside only to find the burly cook standing guard.

"He wants Thomas." Keane tried to explain, but the cook shook his head.

"You talk to him. He doesn't have much time."

Keane's eyes burned as he glared at the man, but the young boy's feeble voice called him back.

"Please, sir. I need to know."

Keane couldn't force himself to turn around.

The boy continued, "Will I go to heaven? I've...I've been awfully...bad."

Keane squeezed his eyes shut. There had been a day when he stood in the pulpit at church and had declared to the young men not to wait to become a child of God. How had he come so far from that message that he now wished someone to go to hell instead? He hurt. He physically hurt from the pain his thoughts brought him. He turned to the boy and sat again on the stool beside the bed. He twisted his hands together, not knowing what to say. Finally, he spoke.

"What's your name?"

"Tommy."

Tommy! The dead face of Tommy Rogers swam before Keane, and he felt sweat roll down his back. A war was being fought inside him. He wanted to shut out of his mind the verses that kept coming to him, but he couldn't. He knew he had to tell this boy the truth. He owed it to Tommy Rogers, and he owed it to this young boy who was about to die. With great effort, he began.

"Tommy, we've all been bad. It's called sin." Keane's voice broke. Who was he to talk to this dying boy? He had declared that he was better than Thorpe Prescott and that if God saved Thorpe, he wanted nothing to do with God. He looked at Tommy's fevered face and pushed on.

"The Bible says that 'there is none righteous. No, not one.' Do you understand that, Tommy?"

"Yes...so then...I...can't go...to heaven?"

"Wait. There's more." Keane's voice shook. "The good news is that Jesus loved us so much, he came to earth and he died for our sins. He forgave us."

Keane stopped. Tears had begun to fall from his eyes and his voice was choked, making it impossible to go on, but Tommy's wheezing prompted him to speak again.

"Then his body was buried. You see, it proved that he had really died. But he rose from the dead, Tommy. That's why he can give us eternal life if we believe that he did this for us. Do you want the forgiveness Jesus offers you, Tommy?"

"Will it mean I...go to heaven?"

"Yes. In fact, it's the only way you can go to heaven. See, we can't be good enough on our own."

Keane waited while Tommy considered his words.

"Can...we be...too...bad?"

Keane put his fist against his mouth to keep a sob from escaping. Isn't that exactly what he thought about Thorpe? That Thorpe was too evil to be saved? But faced with the question from this boy who needed answers, he had to admit the truth that he had known all along.

"No. No, Tommy. Jesus' blood is more powerful than any sin you or I or...*anyone* could ever commit. The Bible says he has forgiven *all* trespasses. That's another word for sin." The very verse Jake had quoted him from Colossians, the one he had scorned, came back to him now in all its truth and grace.

"Tommy, do you believe that Jesus could pay for all your sins by dying on the cross for them?"

The boy's voice was much weaker now. "Yes, sir."

"Do you believe he was buried and that he rose again for you?"

"Yes."

"Then, Tommy, the Bible says you're saved. That means you've become a child of God today."

A smile crossed the boy's face followed by a frown.

"What is it, Tommy?" Keane leaned closer.

"I can't...ever...stop...being his...child, can I?"

Again Keane was struck to his core. "No, you can't. You see, God promises to remain faithful to you, even if you...even if *I*...am not faithful to him. You're his child forever and ever."

"Thank you...for telling...me."

Keane bowed his head and poured out his heart to the Lord in silent prayer as the boy's labored breathing grew weaker.

The curtain was suddenly shoved aside. "Doc's here." The cook announced.

Keane moved out of the way and back into the dining area of the cook shack where he saw Thomas, who was seated at one of the tables. Keane wiped at his eyes before he took the seat across from him. For a moment they just looked at one another.

"Thank you, Thomas."

The words were simple, but they said so much more. The man across from him merely nodded.

Even with his raw emotions exposed, Keane chuckled softly. "You kind of took a chance sending me in there."

"With God all things are possible."

They waited in silence until the doctor came out. The solemn shaking of his head told them all they needed to know. Keane felt his eyes smart with new tears, but they were tears of joy as well. Tommy was with the Lord.

He held out his hand to Thomas and shook it.

"I think I can go home now."

twenty

When Keane got off the train in Ulen, the town was dark with only a few windows sending out welcome light. Night fell early now and activities adjusted accordingly. The residents of the small town were tucked snug and safe in their homes until daybreak was announced.

It was going to be a long, cold, dark walk to the farm. Keane didn't mind the cold, he worked in it every day, and he didn't mind the dark, he knew his way. What made him quicken his pace was that he had been away too long already and was excited, impatient, and anxious to get home, yet he knew the delay getting back from the logging camp had been good for him. It gave him time to think and to reacquaint himself with the grace of God, thanking God over and over for the forgiveness given him at Calvary.

He had walked most of the way already, only catching the train for the last trek of his journey. He wanted to save as much of the money he earned as he could to give his folks and start paying back Jake. People talked along the way of banks failing and hard times coming, especially for farmers. His folks were going to need this money, and he was glad to be able to give it to them.

He thought of Tuva too. He had failed her miserably. She had just gone through that terrible ordeal in the barn and may even have been injured, yet he deserted her, thinking only of himself. Would she ever forgive him? Did he even have a right to court her as he so hoped he could?

He saw the farm now and was glad there were still some light coming from the windows. One light, higher up than the others, was especially bright as if it were right against a window pane, which struck him as odd. His parents didn't usually set a lamp near a cold, dark window. As he got nearer, he saw it was coming from his bedroom, and he stopped to stare at it. The light was for him! It was a light to guide him home!

He was ashamed and humbled. They loved him no matter what, he knew that now. Their love was just a small picture of Christ's love for him despite his failures.

Keane quickened his pace and called out as he approached the house. "Pa! Ma! Jake!"

The door flung open just as he reached it and he was pulled into his father's embrace. Keane felt his mother's arm on his back and welcomed her into the circle. Over their heads and through the tears in his eyes, he saw Jake and heard him say, "Welcome home!"

It was several minutes later before he was seated at the table and Ma was asking if he was hungry.

"No, thank you, Ma. Please just sit and let's talk. I have so much I want…I need to say to you all." He took a deep breath. "First off, Jake, I was terribly rude to you when you came all the way to the logging camp to find me. I apologize for that. After what we've been through together, you'd think I'd know that you were only trying to help me, but one thing, among many that I've learned is that I'm still a sinner and capable of making the worst mistakes. God has had to show me that his grace is more than sufficient, not only in taking away the punishment for *my* sins, but also Thorpe's."

Saying the words came easier than Keane thought, and he meant them. Then he told them about young Tommy.

"I didn't realize how much pride I had, thinking I was better than Thorpe. My friend Thomas—you know, you met him at the camp, Jake—well, he and I had some really good talks after that, and he showed me verse after verse about how wicked and deceitful we all are. When I accepted Christ, I knew I was a sinner and I knew I couldn't do enough good to get to heaven, so it was not difficult for me to accept salvation, but I guess in the back of my mind I always thought that I wasn't really all that bad. And then it was hard for me to understand that even as God's child I was still sinning. Thomas helped me see that until I get to heaven, I still have an old sin nature that will try to rule me. Thankfully, he pointed out that even the sins I may commit tomorrow or next year were forgiven at the cross."

Keane looked down at his folded hands. "I think it will take all eternity for me to comprehend God's goodness and grace to me."

Jake gripped Keane's shoulder. "To all of us, Brother."

"It was wrong of me to leave. I'm sorry for the hurt I've caused you, Ma and Pa."

Thane raised his hand to stop Keane from saying more. "You're back. That's all that matters."

After that Keane asked questions about what occurred after he fled and learned of his mother's role in finding the Rogers and what happened to them. He asked about Mina and her family.

"They had a private funeral for Thorpe, but we asked to attend." Helma explained. "They are at peace about him and so thankful he's with the Lord. They had no animosity for Mr. and Mrs. Rogers, but I think they agreed it was good that they moved on to South Dakota."

"I have some news for you," Jake spoke up. His grin lit his face. "You're going to be best man at my wedding."

Keane was on his feet and clasped Jake in a bear hug. "Congratulations! You and *Mud Girl*, huh? I knew it." He sat down again and looked thoughtful. "Who would have thought when we were on that ship that someday…?" He shook his head in wonder.

The room was quiet for a moment, each with their own thoughts, then Keane spoke again. "And Tuva? How is she?"

Tuva wrapped her scarf about her neck and bundled up in her warmest coat. It was a frosty morning, but there was little wind, so she felt safe in her hike to her favorite tree. She rarely visited what she called her *hiding place* once the cold of winter was firmly upon them, but she longed for the peace and serenity the early morning hours brought her away from the commotion that was unavoidable in a household of eight siblings. It was her time alone with God, where she could pour out her heart to him that often led her to songs of praise.

She smiled to herself at Mina's insistence that she sing a solo in church. She could never do that. It wasn't that she wanted to refuse. It was that she simply would be too nervous. If she knew someone was listening to her, she wouldn't have a voice anymore.

Her thoughts were on Keane every day, so much so that her mother had scolded her for her inattention, yet in a sympathetic way as if she understood the reason. It had taken weeks for Tuva to be able to sleep without reliving the horror of that time in the Wheatly's barn and the fear she felt for the man she loved.

She admitted she loved Keane. Having him leave like he did was as if he had died. She knew he was angry at God and that scared her. She could never align herself with someone who expressed the anger he had toward God, but she still loved him. All she could do was pray that he would remember all he was because of Jesus Christ and come home.

Tuva pulled her scarf closer to her face. She wouldn't be able to stay out long. As was her custom, she looked in all directions before swinging herself onto the bare limb of the tree. There was no shelter from leaves now, no way to hide from prying eyes. Still, she felt she was alone. She looked toward the eastern horizon and waited while she prayed. She never knew what song she was going to sing. It just seemed to come to her.

Her thoughts were on Keane as the first rays appeared, and the words came from her as if she felt her beloved's pain, a pain she shared:

> My soul in sad exile was out on life's sea,
> So burdened with sin and distrest,
> Till I heard a sweet voice saying,
> "Make me your choice;"
> And I entered the "Haven of Rest!"
>
> I've anchored my soul in the "Haven of Rest,"
> I'll sail the wide seas no more;
> The tempest may sweep o'er the wild, stormy deep,
> In Jesus I'm safe evermore.

The sound of her voice seemed to echo across the fields. She whispered, "Thank you, Lord Jesus" as she slid down from the tree to the ground. It was then she felt a presence behind her. She swung around.

"Keane!"

He was standing a short distance away. They both stood entirely still until Tuva took a step toward him. It was what he must have been waiting for, as he began to walk toward her. Tuva couldn't believe her eyes. She started running, as did he, until they were face-to-face.

"Your song was beautiful." Were his first words.

"You heard?"

"I've missed hearing them. I love every one."

"Every…one? You've been here before?"

Keane nodded. He was staring at her as if he were memorizing her features.

Tuva waited. She knew he had something to say, and she was anxious to hear it, yet scared at the same time. He must have known it.

"Don't be afraid of me, Tuva. I'm here to apologize. I never should have run off, and I never should have questioned the justice of an Almighty God."

It was all she needed. She threw her arms around him, and felt his arms encircle her.

"I don't deserve your forgiveness, Tuva. I left you at a most distressful time when you needed my support. I can't promise you I won't fail again. If I've learned anything from this, it is that I have a lot to learn about God and about life. I wonder if you'd be willing to take that learning journey with me. I know it's too soon to talk of marriage, but I want to court you and get to know you."

He paused and Tuva understood that he was giving her time to respond. She pulled back and looked into his face. "I would like that too, Keane."

Keane held her close once again. "I missed you so much, Tuva. I have a lot I need to tell you, but I know you need to get home. May I walk you back and perhaps speak to your father about courting you?"

"Yes, please."

"And you have a lot to tell me. I want to know everything that has happened to you and every song you sang when I wasn't here to listen."

"I never knew you were here before. I never saw you."

"You don't mind, do you? I had to hear your songs. This one you sang today, you sang it for me or because of me, didn't you? I never heard it before, but I don't think I'll ever forget it."

Tuva had her hand tucked into Keane's arm as they walked. "It is a new hymn. I never know what song will come to me, but, yes, I was thinking of you. If I had known you were listening, I don't think I would have been able to sing. I can't seem to sing if I know someone is listening."

"God's listening."

Tuva stopped walking. "I never thought of it that way."

They continued on, and Keane told of his talk with little Tommy and how it showed him his own selfishness and pride. Tuva had tears in her eyes as he shared that Tommy accepted the Lord before he died.

"When did you get home?"

"Last night. I think Jake and my folks and I stayed up most of the night talking."

"And you're up early?"

"I had to know you were all right."

Keane stopped and turned toward Tuva. He bent forward and gently kissed her.

"I love you, Tuva."

Tuva's eyes were shining in response.

"I thought of your eyes a lot when I was away. I couldn't forget them. The only other time I've seen that color is in the glacier waters. The water there is so cold that...not that your eyes are cold, Tuva. I didn't mean it that way. What I mean is—Tuva, are you laughing at me?"

Tuva smiled.

"Yes, I am."

Keane was welcomed into the Thomsen's home amidst a chaotic scene. The toddler called Viktor ran to him and threw his chubby little arms around his knees, nearly causing Keane to fall forward. Three other small children raced by, screaming about someone's shoe being missing. Mrs. Thomsen spoke over the commotion.

"It's good to see you, Keane. Won't you come in? I just put the coffee on."

"Uh, is Mr. Thomsen about?" Keane raised his voice to be heard. "I'd like a word with him."

"He's in the barn doing chores. Would you care to wait?"

"Uh. No, thank you. If it's all right, I'll go out and talk with him there." Keane untangled the boy's arms from his legs and turned to Tuva who was having trouble meeting his eyes. His guess was that laughter was lurking somewhere in her gorgeous eyes. He stepped out the door and Tuva followed.

"Keane, I'm sorry about that. The children are really well behaved, it's just that in the morning…"

"I think I see now why you go out to that tree."

Tuva smiled and nodded.

"Well, I'm off to speak to your father. May I see you this evening then?"

Tuva looked over her shoulder at the house before she spoke. "You think you dare come back?"

Her teasing was a surprise. "Nothing could stop me." He smiled. "I missed you." He reached for her hand but noticed several faces pressed against the window watching them. "Uh, I better go and let you get back inside. Tonight then?"

"Yes."

Keane made his way to the barn with a whistle on his lips. The tune from Tuva's song was still on his mind and some of the words came back to him. He'd have to ask her to sing it again.

Mr. Thomsen was forking hay to the cows.

"Good morning, sir."

Tuva's father stopped and squinted at the newcomer. The dimness of the barn must have made it difficult for him to see Keane, so Keane spoke again.

"It's Keane Wheatly, sir." He stepped forward and held out his hand.

Mr. Thomsen shook hands and looked Keane over carefully. Keane was aware of the scrutiny and waited patiently.

"You're out mighty early."

Something was wrong. The words weren't unfriendly, but they weren't welcoming either. Nervousness crept into Keane's voice.

"Uh, yes, sir. Do you have a minute to talk, sir?"

Mr. Thomsen forked more hay. "About Tuva?"

Relief washed over Keane. "Yes, sir. I'd like your permission to court her, sir."

The farmer kept on with his chores in silence while Keane waited, his apprehension growing.

"Sir, I love your daughter."

Mr. Thomsen stopped his work, the pitchfork still in his hand. "Love? You say you love her? She was almost killed because of you."

"Sir, I—"

"And then for weeks after she couldn't sleep. She had nightmares. And where were you? You took off and left her."

Keane felt himself tremble at the man's words. "I was wrong."

Mr. Thomsen set the fork aside and reached for a bucket.

"God showed me his grace, sir. I ask for the same from you."

The man stopped and looked at Keane. "I can't give it. She's my daughter and she deserves better. She needs someone who will not run out on her when things go bad."

"But—"

"I've said all I need to say. You best go now."

Keane was stunned. Mr. Thomsen turned his back on him and began milking a cow. Keane left the barn, dazed and feeling as though he had been beaten in a fist fight. He had to walk past the house to get to the road, and he saw Tuva in the window watching him. She lifted a hand to wave and he raised his in reply. He saw her turn from the window.

Soon the door opened and she stood there on the porch with a shawl wrapped around her shoulders, her braided hair crowning her head. She was beautiful.

"What's wrong, Keane? What did father say?"

Keane shook his head. "He doesn't trust me. He said you deserve better. He's probably right, but I love you, Tuva. I'm not going anywhere. Somehow I'll prove that to your father. Until then, he won't let me call on you."

"What!"

"I can't say that I blame him. He loves you too, and he wants what's best for you. I can't go against his wishes. I...I don't have the right, but I'm asking you to wait for me, Tuva. Wait until I have your father's approval again. Please?"

"You know I will. Oh, Keane, I'm so sorry."

Keane nodded. He was about to say more when Mr. Thomsen appeared in the doorway of the barn.

"I better go. Good-bye, Tuva."

Keane walked back to the farm with a heavy heart. He hadn't expected to be rejected by the Thomsens, and it hurt to know that Tuva was going to suffer again because of him and his decisions.

"It's no more than I deserve, I guess," he admitted to his family later. "I knew there would be consequences for my actions, but I hadn't anticipated this."

"Well, it's a crying shame!" Helma exclaimed. "Ole Thomsen has known you since you were a little boy. How dare he forbid you to court his daughter!"

"It's his right." Thane put in. "Give him time, Keane. He just needs to know you're dependable now. I don't have a daughter, but I might just feel the same way."

Seeing it like that, Keane had to agree. "But how do I convince him?"

"Keep on living for the Lord, son. Live for him, not for the respect of others."

Jake was sympathetic to Keane's plight. They worked together on repairs to the Zimmerman house that would soon be home to him and Mina, and they renewed the friendship that had upheld them throughout their trials.

"I ran off and married Eva without approval from my family. She had no family to get approval from, but I would have been devastated if I had been refused." Jake chuckled. "Although in my rebellious state, I may have stolen her away anyway. Not that you should with Tuva." He added hastily.

Keane's laugh was without humor. "No. I wouldn't do that. It's hard to be patient though. I read God's Word and it sustains me." He shook off his gloom. "I think Mina will like what we've done. What do you think?" He changed the subject.

"Yep. As soon as we finish taking out this wall, she wants to get in here and do some work too. By the way, now that you're home, we're thinking of moving the wedding up to around Christmas. You okay with that?"

"Sure! I didn't know you were waiting on me."

"I needed a best man, remember?"

Keane smiled. "Tuva's standing up for Mina, isn't she? I bet she'll be beautiful. At least I'll get to stand with her and see her." Keane had a far off look in his eyes.

Jake sighed. "Okay, lover boy, come back out of the clouds. There's some floor boards here that are loose."

Keane tried to fill the days by keeping busy helping Jake with carpentry work and doing the chores on the farm. The winter's work wasn't as hectic, but there were still plenty of things to do, and Keane found his father was giving more and more of it over to him. Keane was glad to take the load off his aging father and mother.

He looked forward to Sundays. Between Jake and the present pastor the sermons were edifying and instructive. Keane hungered for the Word and often studied with Jake. But Sundays also meant he got to see Tuva, if only from a distance. Her smile held a sadness that made his heart ache, but he always tried to give her an encouraging one in return.

After each Sunday service Keane made it a practice of speaking to Tuva's father and making his request to court Tuva again. Each time the man gave a negative shake of his head. Keane left it at that, thanked the man for his time, and returned to his wagon and waiting family. He knew others in town had become aware of the stand-off between him and

Tuva's father and it was the talk of some gossip in the small town, but he didn't mind. He would continue to ask until Tuva's father gave permission.

Tuva didn't sing in the mornings any longer. Keane went religiously every day, but she never came. He was sure her father forbade her, and that was another infliction on her that was Keane's fault. He knew how much Tuva needed time away by herself and now because of him, she was denied that as well.

Christmas was coming, and Jake and Mina announced that their wedding would take place Christmas Day.

"Everyone will be at the church for the service anyway, so it seemed a good time to have the ceremony and some refreshments before people go home to celebrate the holiday." Jake's excitement was contagious, and Keane couldn't be happier for his friend. Having him live so close by was another benefit.

Keane and Jake came in from chores, shaking the snow and cold from their coats. Jake took a step into the house and stopped, wrinkling his nose.

"What's that smell? Is there a dead rat somewhere?"

Helma came from the kitchen and put her hands on her hips. "Jake Rodwell, you cut that out! You know I'm soaking lutefisk."

For days Helma had been doing her Christmas baking and explaining to Jake the Norwegian foods they all enjoyed at this time of year. Jake had no problem with fattigmand. At Mina's request, he had brought her to learn the traditional Christmas baking from Helma. Together the women had prepared a dough, shaped it, and dipped it in butter and fried it on an iron in deep fat, then sprinkled it with powdered sugar. It was delicious.

He also liked krumkake. Helma had a special griddle that made designs on the thin, waffle-like pastries. Mina was fun to watch as she shaped the warm discs into cones, often breaking them in her first tries. Jake didn't mind because he got to eat the broken pieces. When the cones were formed, the ladies filled them with sweet cream.

Even though lefse was an oddity to Jake, he found that the thin, flat pancake made from potatoes was quite good when buttered and sprinkled with sugar. He laughed as Mina tried her hand at flipping the large, round disc on the griddle with a flat, wooden stick. He even tried his hand at it.

"When will we have to eat that fish?" Jake asked, holding his nose.

Keane grinned at his friend. "It's not as bad as it smells, trust me."

"Oh, you two!" Helma put out some krumkake with coffee for the men as they washed their hands. "It's soaked long enough now, so I will cook it tonight for our supper. I bought enough dried lutefisk from the store to have it again on Christmas Eve. That's tradition, you know."

Jake stepped over to the basin where the whitefish was soaking. The gelatinous fish had swelled during its days of soaking. "My eyes are watering!" He exclaimed. "How can you possibly eat this?"

"You'll see." Helma was undaunted. "You'll love it."

"You're going to serve it on the night before my wedding?" Jake shook his head. "Probably good that we're having a trial run tonight."

Keane chuckled.

"Of course, all your cooking is so good, Helma. I'm not really worried. You know I'm just teasing you."

Keane hid a smile.

"Like that stuff you made for breakfast. What was that called? You know, that mush with the cinnamon and sugar and melted butter."

"Rommegrot." Helma smiled her pleasure. "I'm glad you like it. Mina has all the recipes and she's getting quite good at her cooking."

"Good to hear. Otherwise, I might have to sneak over here for a meal now and then."

The others laughed.

It was later when the men were putting away their tools at Jake's future house before going in for supper that Thane made a comment to Keane.

"You've gotten pretty good at carpentry. How did you learn to do this?"

Keane explained about building the cook shack and working with the carpenter at the logging camp. "I learned a lot from him, and I like doing it."

Thane nodded. "That cabinet you put in Mina's kitchen will certainly please her. I was wondering, how would you feel about building a little house over by your ma's strawberry patch?"

"A house? Why?"

"I was thinking your Ma and I could use some space of our own when you and Tuva are married. You young people can have the house."

Keane stared at his father.

"Married? I'm not even allowed to see Tuva!"

"I'm not thinking we need a lot of room." Thane continued as if Keane hadn't spoken. "But we'll want some privacy and so will you. It would be good to have a little distance between us to block off some of the noise once you start having children. Babies can be kind of loud."

Jake was grinning at Keane as he raised his eyebrows at Thane.

"Pa, I think you're getting a little ahead of yourself."

"Your Ma might like a cabinet like that for herself. She just needs a small kitchen for the two of us. For big meals, we can always join you and Tuva, can't we?"

"Yes, I mean, I don't know! Pa!"

Thane put on his hat. "Better get home, boys. Ma has lutefisk!"

Keane looked at Jake after his father left Jake's house. "What was that all about?"

Jake shrugged. "He kept saying he knew you were coming home when you were away at the logging camp. He was confident, and he was right. He seems pretty sure of himself about you and Tuva. Do you mind sharing the land with your folks?"

Keane slipped on his coat. "No, of course not. I always planned on something like that, but this is crazy. He can't count on Tuva marrying me. I can't even be sure it's going to happen."

"Well, let's not worry about it tonight. Let's go eat fish. I'm hungry!"

Jake's face after his first bite of lutefisk had the members of the Wheatly family in tears from laughing so hard.

Keane speared a piece of the jelly-like substance, dipped it in melted butter, and popped it into his mouth while he grinned at Jake who was trying to swallow.

"It slips all over in my mouth!" Jake grabbed his glass of milk and downed it.

Thane chuckled as he rolled some lutefisk in his lefse and bit into it.

"Does that work?" Jake watched him. He looked at the lefse on his plate and then at the lutefisk. "No, I don't think so. Helma, please tell me you didn't give the recipe for lutefisk to Mina."

Helma laughed as she got up from the table. "At least you tried it, Jake. I'll give you credit for that." She went to the kitchen and came back with a plate of roast beef. "Here you go, Jake. I didn't want you to starve."

"Bless you, Helma!"

Jake helped himself to the offering then watched the others devour the plate of lutefisk. "How can you eat it?" he asked. His question revealed that he honestly didn't understand.

Keane dished himself another helping. "I think it's because we grew up with it. We're used to it. I like it."

"Okay. I'll give it another try." They all stopped to watch as Jake dipped the wobbly fish into the butter then held it up as if inspecting it. He took a deep breath and dropped it into his mouth. He swirled it from side to side, making faces as he did so before dramatically swallowing it. Again he grabbed for his glass of milk while the others laughed.

"Please pass the roast beef."

twenty-one

Jake was nearly frozen from his walk to town. He stood in the lobby of the City Hotel, trying to warm himself as he waited for Mina. They were going to spend the first part of Christmas Eve with her family, and then he was going to return to the Wheatlys to celebrate with them while Mina and her family had some time alone before tomorrow's wedding. He turned from the fireplace when he heard her on the stairs. Her beauty struck him again as she hurried toward him, but it was the love in her eyes that made his heart beat faster. How thankful he was that he was given another opportunity to love and be loved!

"Jake, you look so cold. Maybe you shouldn't have walked here today. Can't you take the sleigh home? I worry so about you."

Jake pulled her into an embrace and kissed her.

"One more day and you'll be my wife." He brushed aside her concerns with a smile. "Do you think we're crazy getting married on Christmas Day?"

"We would be crazy not to." Mina laughed. "Oh, Jake! I'm so happy! Only..."

"Only what? What is it?"

Mina bit her lower lip. "I worry about Tuva. Jake, she's so unhappy. She never says anything about Keane, but I know she's in love with him. I wish we could help them."

"Now, hold on." Jake led Mina to the nearby settee. "We can't interfere. You know that. Keane won't go against Mr. Thomsen's wishes and cause division in their family, so you and I certainly cannot."

"Oh, I know. It just seems wrong for me to be so happy when my friend isn't."

"The way you care about others touches my heart, but right now it's your happiness I'm concerned about. Let's leave Keane and Tuva to God and concentrate right now on our wedding. Is there anything else that I need to do?"

"Yes." Mina smiled. "You have to say 'I do'."

Jake grinned then said solemnly. "I do." He was about to kiss her again when they were interrupted by a voice calling from the dining room.

"Mina! Mina, did I hear Jake arrive?"

Mina sighed then giggled at Jake's expression. "Yes, Mother!"

"Well, bring him in. Everything's ready."

"Coming, Mother!" Mina stood and pulled Jake to his feet. "Come. I can't wait for you to see what Mother and I have fixed for dinner."

"Please tell me it's not lutefisk."

"Goodness, no! Father got a turkey, so it's turkey dinner with all the trimmings."

Jake picked Mina up and twirled her about the room.

"Thank you!"

Christmas Day dawned clear and cold. Mina looked out at the sky and breathed a sigh of relief that there were no clouds threatening snow. It looked like travel would be possible for the many families who would come to the Christmas service and the wedding.

From her seat by the window she turned to look again at the white dress spread across her bed, waiting for her to don. It was a simple dress, but elegant because of its simplicity. Her father had recently rented the sample room to a dressmaker and milliner, which turned out to be fortuitous for Mina, who took advantage of having the dress made right there in the hotel, along with other garments to complete her trousseau. Despite the attraction of some of the fancier outfits the dressmaker tempted her with, Mina made practical choices. She was under no illusions that her life as a farmer's wife and preacher's wife would require such elaborate clothing. She was perfectly happy in the role she was about to undertake.

Mina checked the clock. Tuva would be arriving soon. Tuva's dress hung neatly on a hanger, and Mina walked over to finger the soft, velvet material. *This deep green color will go so well with Tuva's eyes.*

Mina heard voices in the lobby of the hotel and waited impatiently for Tuva to join her. She was nervous and excited at the same time, hardly able to eat the breakfast her mother prepared for her that morning.

Mina opened the door to her room and stepped out before Tuva had completed ascending the stairway. "Tuva! Merry Christmas! Come in!" She hugged her friend before Tuva could even remove her coat. "I thought you'd never get here! Oh, Tuva! I'm so happy!" Mina spun around the room in her delight.

"And I'm happy for you. You are going to be a beautiful Christmas bride. The dining room looks so pretty. You and your mother have obviously been very busy preparing the refreshments. Oh, your dress is lovely!" Tuva went to the bed and examined the fine work without touching the garment. "It turned out just as you hoped, and mine?" She looked about the room until she spotted it. "It's gorgeous, Mina! That seamstress is very talented, but after today, I don't know when I will ever wear such a fancy dress again."

Mina motioned for Tuva to join her by the window seat. "You'll have lots of occasions to wear it, I'm sure. Tuva, are you okay? Is today going to be difficult for you, I mean, with Keane and all? Oh dear, I didn't say that very well, did I?"

Tuva smiled at her friend. "It's your wedding day. You're allowed to say whatever you want." She looked out the frosty glass of the window. "I won't lie and say it will be easy to see Keane standing beside Jake. It's been so hard, not being allowed to visit with him." She turned to Mina. "Did you know that Keane asks Father every week for permission to court me?" She looked out the window again. "And every week Father says no."

Mina nodded. "Yes, I knew. I'm so sorry, Tuva."

"Yesterday Ole Hanson came to the house and spoke with Father. When Father told me that Ole wanted permission to call on me, I said no. I told him it was Keane or no one."

"You did? Oh, Tuva! What did your father say?"

"He said I should be a dutiful daughter and obey, and I told him I had obeyed him and that I was miserable and that I would not marry anyone but Keane, even if that meant being a spinster the rest of my life."

"Oh!" For a moment Mina stared at Tuva in awe then she giggled. "Oh, I would have loved to have been there to hear that!"

Tuva was surprised at Mina's reaction then she began to laugh. "I shouldn't have done it, but he has to know how I feel."

Mina patted her hand. "He'll come around. He has to."

By the time Mr. Prescott called for the girls, they were ready to be taken to the church. Mrs. Prescott joined them in the lobby, dabbing at her eyes.

"Mother! No tears! This is the happiest day of my life!" Mina scolded.

"My little girl!" Mrs. Prescott sniffed, making Tuva and Mina hide smiles from one another.

They had waited to arrive until the last minute just as the Christmas service got underway. Jake and Keane stood at the back of the church and met them as the Prescotts led the girls into the building.

"Jake! You shouldn't see Mina yet!" Mrs. Prescott stood in front of her daughter like a shield.

Mina intervened. "No, Mother. Remember? We're all going forward *together* after the service. It's okay." Mina tried to see Jake around her mother.

"No, it's not okay. You two men go sit down and don't you dare turn around." Mrs. Prescott whispered the warning with such authority that Jake and Keane could not refuse to obey. They sat down, but Keane turned and caught Tuva's eye. He smiled, and Mina watched as Tuva sent him an unveiled look of love in return.

"You girls take off your coats and stay out here in the vestibule. I'll stand guard."

"Mother! Stand guard?" Mina turned to her father. "What is she doing?"

Mr. Prescott took one look at his wife's face. "Best do as she says, girls." His look of long suffering was almost Tuva and Mina's undoing. They muffled their laughter and were silenced completely by a look from Mrs. Prescott.

"I thought we had this all planned," Tuva whispered to Mina.

"Me too. I guess Mother has other ideas." She shrugged and grinned. Nothing was going to bother her today.

They listened quietly to the music going on in the other room. Tuva hummed along under her breath to the Christmas carol, and Mina nudged her. "You should be singing a solo today for my wedding."

Tuva made a face at her, making Mina laugh again. She thought of the look between Keane and Tuva she had witnessed.

"Thank you for doing this for me, Tuva. I hope I get to stand up for you at your wedding." Her whisper was for Tuva's ears only.

Tuva raised her eyebrows in question. "Do you know something I don't know?"

"I know true love when I see it."

Tuva's blush was her answer.

As the Christmas service was ending, Tuva found herself getting nervous. She heard the pastor explain that the wedding was to take place next, and he called for Jake and Keane to step to the front.

"Okay, girls. Mina, do you have your Bible ready?" Mina nodded. She carried a small, white Bible bedecked with ribbons. There were no flowers in December, so Tuva held a small bouquet of flowing ribbons in place of them. "Tuva will start down the aisle once the music begins." Mrs. Prescott took Tuva's arm and directed her to stand ready.

Tuva spoke to Mina over her shoulder. "I didn't know I had to do this!" Panic was in her voice, so Mina tried to calm her down.

"You'll be fine. I didn't know either, but you'll be okay. Just look at Keane."

Tuva felt Mrs. Prescott give her a little shove. She didn't budge.

"Tuva, the music is playing. You have to walk to the front now!" Mrs. Prescott's whisper was a command.

With another nudge from behind, Tuva took the first step, then the second. People were looking at her and she began to tremble, the ribbon bouquet shaking in her hands. Mina's words to look at Keane made her look up, and there he was looking right at her and smiling. Tuva smiled back and kept her eyes on him the rest of the way. The pastor pointed to where she should stand or Tuva would have walked right into Keane's arms. Once in position she was aware that the people were standing up for the bride's entrance. It gave her another moment to look at Keane. The look that passed between them revealed the love they had for one another. Tuva took a deep breath to steady herself.

She was barely aware of the others in the room as she heard the marriage vows exchanged between Mina and Jake. She repeated the vows in her mind as if she and Keane were the bride and groom standing before the preacher. She glanced at the couple as they sealed their vows with a kiss before the congregation and then walked down the aisle together. The preacher was saying something about everyone gathering at the hotel for refreshments when she saw Keane step forward and hold out his arm to her. It was only then that she realized he was going to escort her after the newlyweds.

Tuva stepped forward and took Keane's arm. Her eyes never left his as they walked together. She was completely unaware of the knowing looks of the people watching. She saw only Keane.

"You are stunning, Tuva. I can only hope and pray that soon, very soon I will be making you my bride." Keane's words were for her ears only.

"That would make me very happy, Keane."

Keane helped Tuva on with her coat but instead of joining the Prescotts and Jake and Mina in the sleigh that was to take them back to the hotel, Keane told them that he and Tuva would walk. Tuva smiled as Mrs. Prescott acknowledged what Keane said even though Jake and Mina seemed oblivious to anyone but themselves.

Keane took Tuva's hand and tucked it into his arm again. "I want to keep you to myself as long as possible, even though I am risking the wrath of your father to do so."

Tuva glanced back at the church. "It will take them some time to gather all the children." She smiled at Keane. "I have missed you. Please tell me everything you've been doing."

"I'd rather tell you how much I love you and want to marry you."

Tuva nodded. "I wish...I wish you could." She cleared her throat. "Are your folks well? I only see them on Sundays now. I miss visiting with your mother."

"Tuva." Keane pulled her with him to the side of a building. He held her close for a moment then kissed her. "I had to do that. Ever since you stepped into the church, I knew I had to kiss you today."

Tuva buried herself in his arms once more then stepped away. "We must go."

"I know. But you need to know I'll wait, Tuva. I'll wait as long as it takes."

"So will I." It was a promise.

They hurried on to the hotel and joined the others who were beginning to gather. Ladies from the church quickly took over serving so that the Prescotts and the newlyweds could visit with their guests. Tuva stepped over to stand by Mina.

"Congratulations, Mr. and Mrs. Rodwell." She gently hugged Mina so as not to mess her hair then turned to Jake who enveloped her in a bear hug. Blushing, Tuva laughed. "I'd say you're a happy man today."

"Yes I am!"

Keane joined them and Jake shook the hand he extended.

The next hour was a strain for Tuva. She visited and helped and served and all the while was aware of Keane watching her. Having him so close and not being able to talk freely with him was torture. When the newlyweds departed for their home, the crowd started to disperse and Tuva saw her mother signal her that they would be leaving soon.

"I just need to get my things from Mina's room then I'll be ready," she told her mother. Tuva climbed the stairs and gathered up the belongings she brought with her. As she descended the staircase, she saw Keane waiting at the bottom. She looked around quickly for her family but no one was in sight.

Keane smiled at her. "I couldn't let you leave without your Christmas present, Miss Thomsen," he said formally.

"A present?"

He handed her a small box. "A present and a promise, if you will accept it. Please open it when you are alone."

Tuva kept her eyes on his while she slipped the box into her pocket. "Thank you, Keane. Merry Christmas. I...I have something for you too." Tuva pulled a flat package from her bag and handed it to him. "I know it's not much. It's the words to that hymn you liked so well."

"Thank you. I will treasure it, and I'll hear your voice singing it when I read it."

"Well, good-bye."

Tuva stepped toward the door.

"I spoke to your father again." Keane stopped her with his words. She turned in anticipation, but he shook his head. She nodded in understanding.

Her father was waiting when she came out the door but she didn't look at him as he helped her into the sleigh. Her brothers and sisters talked nonstop about the wedding and the food and peppered her with questions she only half-heartedly answered. It was a relief when she could finally get to the room she shared with two of her sisters. Even then she had to wait until they changed out of their church clothes before she could have the room to herself. She sat on the bed and brushed the soft velvet of her dress before opening her hand with the gift from Keane nestled inside. She dared not let her sisters see the gift. Even now she looked at the closed door and decided to stand with her back against it so as not to have someone walk in on her and discover her secret.

She opened the box carefully and had to stifle a gasp with the back of her hand over her mouth. A small, delicate ring tucked into a velvet cocoon sparkled up at her. Keane said it was a present and a promise. Earlier on their walk he said he wanted to marry her. It was a bold thing for him to say in light of her father's continual denial of his request to court her, but the ring was a symbol of his promise to wait for her.

She took the ring out of its case and slipped it on her finger. As much as she wanted to keep it there, she knew she couldn't. There was a necklace she always wore. She quickly unfastened it and slipped the ring on the chain and put it back around her neck. Tucked into her dress it was unnoticeable, but it was there where she could feel it and remember Keane's promise. She felt at peace, a feeling she hadn't had in a long time.

Keane stood in the pulpit the next Sunday morning and smiled at the perplexed faces of the congregation. After the song leader closed the singing service in prayer, he nodded to Keane. It was only then that Keane rose from his seat in the front row and stepped up on the platform, the first indication to the people who the speaker was. Normally the preacher sat in the seat behind the pulpit up on the platform. Today that seat had been empty.

"I see you're surprised. Well, so am I."

He saw some smiles and nods from the people.

"As you know my friend Jake Rodwell will be handling the services for the next months while our pastor is away, and as you also know, Jake and his wife are away on their honeymoon. I was given the great privilege of being asked to fill in for him."

Keane was very aware of Tuva and her family in the third row back on his right. Mr. Thomsen had not smiled in response to Keane's introduction. He sat with his arms folded in front of him and an expression that Keane could only surmise as disapproval.

Keane hadn't wanted this responsibility when Jake asked him, but he gave his apprehension to the Lord and was relying on him to get him through and hopefully to use him to help others.

"I have no right to be up here." His opening words had people sitting up straighter in their seats. "Many of you heard Jake and I speak about our experience at sea. The last time I spoke to you I was fervent in the Lord and praising him for his goodness to me. Then I failed him. I failed my family, and I failed the people who loved me."

Keane did not look at Tuva as he spoke. He had studied and prayed over his message and he wanted God's Word to have an impact on the people, not his own words.

"I have come to know four people named Thomas during my life. I told you about Tommy

Rogers who was on the ship with Jake and me. I'm going to call him 'Desperate Thomas'. Keane retold Tommy's story for his listeners.

"Later when I met Tommy's parents, I learned that Tommy knew the Lord. I could rejoice that he was in heaven and away from the horrors of sin here on earth. And then Mr. and Mrs. Rogers saved my life. They saved Jake's life, and the lives of several other people."

Keane told about their capture in the barn. Even though many knew the man he referred to in his tale was the Prescott's son, he didn't mention him by name. "This man who I still hated with every ounce of my being, this man who had tormented men, tortured men, and even murdered men was given the opportunity to accept the forgiveness of sins, and he placed his faith in Christ's finished work on the cross for him. I should have rejoiced in his salvation, but I did not."

Keane faced the people. "I wanted him to go to the lake of fire and suffer for all eternity." He paused and could feel the tension in the room at his words. "Then I fled. I wanted nothing more to do with people who could forgive this man. I wanted nothing more to do with God.

"That brings me to the next Thomas in my life. I'm going to call him 'Diligent Thomas.' This man is the most annoying, happy, persistent man I've ever met. I hurled the anger I felt toward God right in Thomas's face, but he stood like the soldier in Ephesians 6. He stood fast. He met my every insult, every curse, and every abuse with patience and kindness. He shared God's love with me, he quoted verses, he whistled hymns that stuck in my head until I thought I'd go crazy, and then this diligent man played a trick on me. He sent me to another Thomas."

There was not a sound in the building as Keane continued. "This was 'Dying Thomas.'"

Keane gripped the sides of the pulpit as he faced the congregation and began to tell young Tommy's story and the conversation they had together. "Tommy understood that he couldn't be good enough to go to heaven because he was a sinner, but then he asked me a question that tore at my heart. He asked if it was possible that he could be too bad.

"It was the very thing I had been angry with God about. I felt that my enemy was too sinful to go to heaven because I didn't want him there. What I was actually saying was that I didn't believe the blood of Jesus Christ was sufficient to pay for his sins. When Tommy asked me that question, I was brought to my knees. The verse in Romans 5:20 came immediately to my mind, '...But where sin abounded, grace did much more abound.' I had to tell the boy the truth. In the book of Titus it says that Christ '...gave himself for us, that he might redeem us from *all* iniquity.'

"Tommy believed on the Lord that night, and I rejoice that he is now in heaven with his savior.

"The final Thomas I think you all know. I'm talking about the one we call 'Doubting Thomas' in the book of John. This Thomas refused to believe in Jesus' resurrection until he had visible proof. He did not believe the words of the others who told him what they had seen. I, too, doubted the Lord. I didn't believe his Word when he said, '...him that cometh to me I will in no wise cast out.'

"I've learned a lot from each Thomas in my life, and I thank the Lord for each one of them. It was my pride that made me not want someone to get saved because I thought I was better than that person. The truth is that none of us deserve to go to heaven. It is all by God's grace that any of us can be redeemed through faith in what his Son accomplished on the cross.

"I'd like to close with the words to a song that I have only recently learned. Don't worry, I'm not going to attempt to sing it. These words have meant a lot to me because they reflect what I have been through and how God has given me a safe haven with him. It starts—"

Keane looked up from the paper in his hand when there was a stirring among the people seated before him. He stared at Tuva who had suddenly stood to her feet. She was looking at him as if asking permission. He held her look for a moment, understanding what she was silently asking him, then nodded to her.

Tuva closed her eyes while the room waited in silence. Then she began to sing, filling the room with the beauty of her voice and the message of the words:

My soul in sad exile was out on life's sea,
So burdened with sin and distrest,
Till I heard a sweet voice saying,
"Make me your choice;"
And I entered the "Haven of Rest!"

I've anchored my soul in the "Haven of Rest,"
I'll sail the wide seas no more;
The tempest may sweep o'er the wild, stormy
deep,
In Jesus I'm safe evermore.

The room sat in stunned silence, then a resounding "Amen!" made Tuva open her eyes. Keane could see that she had forgotten where she was as she sang. She sat down with a red blush staining her cheeks, but she still smiled up at Keane.

The song leader concluded the service and Keane moved to the back of the church to shake hands with the people as they left. He was surprised to find Jake and Mina waiting for him there.

"What are you two doing here?"

"We wouldn't have missed hearing you speak." Jake slapped Keane on the back.

"But, if you knew you were going to be here, they why didn't you do the service?"

"Sorry, friend. I'm still on my honeymoon, and if you don't mind, I'm going to sneak my wife out of here and go home before we get waylaid. Great job, great message. Praise the Lord!" Jake started to pull Mina along with him, but his wife stopped before Keane.

"I've tried to get Tuva to sing in church. How did you manage it? Wasn't she wonderful! I had tears in my eyes."

Before Keane could answer, Jake swept Mina away. Keane laughed at them before turning to greet the other parishioners. He appreciated the kind words he received as he shook hands and thanked people for being there, all the while he was waiting to see Tuva. Her song was mentioned by everyone, and he was sure she was being surrounded by people who were thanking her for sharing her gift of song with them today.

The church had about emptied out when Mr. Thomsen stepped up to Keane and held out his hand. He said nothing, but he waited as if he expected Keane to speak. This was a surprise, for every Sunday for the last several weeks the man had tried to avoid contact with Keane, knowing what question he wanted to ask.

Something was different today. Keane looked the man in the eye and said, "Mr. Thomsen, I'd like your permission to court your daughter."

"You have it on one condition." Mr. Thomsen's voice was gruff.

Keane's heart began to beat faster. "Name it, sir."

"You need to accept my apology first."

"Sir?"

"Keane, what you said today struck me at my heart. I have been holding your sin against you, and I had no right. My pride made me think I was better than you. Thank the Lord he has forgiven us both. Then when Tuva sang...I never heard her sing like that. Oh, she hums and sings a little around the house, but not like she did today with her heart full of love for the Lord...and for you."

Keane was shaking Mr. Thomsen's hand before the man finished speaking. "Thank you, sir. Excuse me, please." He raced into the church to look for Tuva.

She was waiting for him. She sat in the front row, her head bowed, but when she heard his footsteps she turned and stood to her feet. "Did Father tell you?" Her face was beaming with happiness.

"Yes! May I see you home? Oh, wait! My folks will have the sleigh. You could ride with us and I could drop them off and then see you home or—"

"Or we could walk."

Keane took a deep breath then released it. "Or we could walk. Miss Thomsen?" He held out his arm. Tuva smiled and tucked her hand into it.

"Thank you for singing."

Tuva and Keane were married in the spring. The whole community gathered for the outdoor service. Jake officiated. Thane was best man, and Mina, with a new life growing inside her, got her wish to stand with her best friend. Helma cried with happiness.

Thomas came from the logging camp. The Rogers sat beside the Prescotts. All eight of Tuva's siblings sat in the front row with their mother and father. Ten-year-old Ole Jasperson caught the bouquet.

And Tuva sang.

References

Black, James M. *When the Roll is Called Up Yonder,* 1893. Melody by James M. Black. *Living Hymns,* Grand Rapids, MI: Zondervan Publishing House, 1967, p. 396. Public Domain.

Centennial Book Committee. *Spanning the Century– The History of Ulen, Minnesota 1886-1986.* Ulen, MN: *The Ulen Union,* 1985.

Gilmour, Henry L. *The Haven of Rest,* 1890. Melody by George D. Moore. *Living Hymns,* Grand Rapids, MI: Zondervan Publishing House, 1967, p. 284. Public Domain.

Newton, John. *Amazing Grace,* 1779. Unknown Author. *Verse 7,* 1829. *Living Hymns,* Grand Rapids, MI: Zondervan Publishing House, 1967, p. 385. Public Domain.

Raun, Agnes Lunde. *Pioneer Daughter-Memories of growing up on the prairies of Minnesota with my parents Swen and Ingeborg (Sylte) Lunde.* Complied by Eldora Lunde, 1993.

75 Years of Progress-Ulen Diamond Jubilee 1886-1961. Ulen, MN, 1961.

Watts, Isaac. *When I Survey the Wondrous Cross,* 1707. Melody by Lowell Mason. . *Living Hymns,* Grand Rapids, MI: Zondervan Publishing House, 1967, p.130. Public Domain.

Other books by
Author Margo Hansen

A Newly Weds Series:
Sky's Bridal Train
Jade's Courting Danger
Emma's Marriage Secret
Irena's Bond of Matrimony
Mattie's Unspoken Vow

Tall Timber Trilogy:
Greatly Beloved
Only Beloved
Brother Beloved

MARGO HANSEN, author of *A Newly Weds Series* and *Tall Timber Trilogy,* loves writing about the north woods of Minnesota where she lives with her husband Bruce. Her greatest desire is to share the Gospel of God's Grace with others through her stories.

For more information about
Author Margo Hansen:

www.margohansen.com

Margo would enjoy hearing
from her readers.
Send your questions or comments to:

margo@margohansen.com

Made in the USA
Monee, IL
01 March 2022